PRAISE FOR *SUTURE*

"*Suture* is Nic Brewer's transgressively taut storytelling.
The notes in these pages write desire, connection and
art from the body's vivid capacity for tenderness where
the hard stuff tears. A nimble, fearless debut."

CANISIA LUBRIN,
AUTHOR OF *THE DYZGRAPHXST*

"*Suture* is a daring, visceral debut that examines
the painful side of the creative process. Blending
body horror with meditations on love, art, and
forgiveness, this novel will startle and captivate you."

CATRIONA WRIGHT,
AUTHOR OF *DIFFICULT PEOPLE*

"I read this book with wonder—Brewer's confident
prose swept me along. Hers is sure, sharp writing
that doesn't flinch from tenderness. I felt this book in my
body. I ached (in my heart and bones, along an old,
spidery scar that split my chest in two) long after
I set it down. What a privilege to read this work."

GILLIAN WIGMORE,
AUTHOR OF *GLORY*

Suture

Sut

Nic Brewer

ure

Book*hug Press

Toronto 2021

Library and Archives Canada Cataloguing in Publication

Title: Suture / Nic Brewer.
Names: Brewer, Nic, author.
Identifiers: Canadiana (print) 2021025985x | Canadiana (ebook)
20210259892
    ISBN 9781771667029 (softcover)
    ISBN 9781771667036 (EPUB)
    ISBN 9781771667043 (PDF)
Classification: LCC PS8603.R74 S88 2021 | DDC C813/.6—dc23

The production of this book was made possible through the generous
assistance of the Canada Council for the Arts and the Ontario Arts Council.
Book*hug Press also acknowledges the support of the Government of
Canada through the Canada Book Fund and the Government of Ontario
through the Ontario Book Publishing Tax Credit and the Ontario Book Fund.

 Canada Council
for the Arts
Conseil des Arts
du Canada

Book*hug Press acknowledges that the land on which we operate is
the traditional territory of many nations, including the Mississaugas
of the Credit, the Anishnabeg, the Chippewa, the Haudenosaunee,
and the Wendat peoples. We recognize the enduring presence of many
diverse First Nations, Inuit, and Métis peoples and are grateful for
the opportunity to meet, work, and learn on this territory.

For Tab,
and for anyone who needs it.
I love you.

A map of
your journey

*T*he women were three storeys tall and the police were trying to shatter the crowd. They couldn't find the projector. So these twenty-foot-tall cunts and bushes played the whole time, right on the side of the station. The baton sticks so appropriately phallic while these ghostly Amazonian women sat naked and read police reports to each other over a pot of peppermint tea. Some days I hate that that's my legacy: cunts and bushes and a blushing riot. Imagine, your edgy undergrad thesis haunting you for the rest of your career. I love it, I love what we did...but I wish it didn't show up on every list of great feminist film projects. They have all been feminist, you know? Not just the one with naked giantesses.

A woman falls in love with women.

My right eye was still in the camera when they arrested me. They knocked off the eye patch when they pushed me into the back—you should have seen it. Have you? An empty eye socket? It's disgusting. Everyone thinks it's going to be black, but they don't remember the blood. It crusts under the eye patch after a while, this ring of scabby brown right where your makeup would smudge. Clumping the eyelashes. And the eyelid sags dreadfully, with the extra weight of the blood, the eyelashes. Into the concavity, a little wrinkly, too soft without the eye there to support it. But if you lift it up out of the way, the inside is more white than anything. A slick white with smears of the brightest red. Not like when you bleed; brighter. Almost translucent. Shiny. It's not dark at all in the socket—it's eerily light. Light and wet.

A woman falls in love with injustice.

People started yelling "cunt" at me everywhere I went. It felt like I had accomplished something.

A woman falls in love with rage.

I learned to fight after the third time someone tried to take my eyes.

A woman falls in love with justice.

My aunt's best friend gave me her son's camera for my thirteenth birthday, but she didn't tell me how to use it. She didn't tell me anything. Her son had killed himself at film school a few months earlier, and how do you tell someone that? Maybe the way I just told you, or maybe you hand over a used $3,000 video camera and say "careful, honey," and "sorry we don't have the box anymore," and you let the memory harden just a little bit more and you hope it doesn't happen again. This was before the internet, remember. There was nowhere for me to go to learn how to use a real camera. But there was a movie being filmed just around the corner from my friend's house that summer, and I snuck onto the set every day to try to catch the directors in the act. Eventually I saw them, calmly popping their eyes into their palms, slipping them into their cameras; there was a lot more blood when I tried it.

A woman falls in love with potential.

I went blind for the first time shortly after I had finally mastered taking my eyes out and getting them back in. Now I was ready to use the camera, I thought. But cameras are custom made, and this one was custom made for a dead kid. I shoved my eyes into the battery slot and started filming. I pointed it ahead of me and turned in a circle in the middle of my room. A crushing pain in the back of my head cut the adventure short, my view dark around the edges and getting darker. When I took my eyes out of the camera, they were smaller, wrinkled, almost dented in places. And when I put them back into my own sockets, I couldn't see anything but a soft, borderless grey. Shapes appeared after an hour, blurry and greyscale, sharpening slowly; I didn't move the entire time.

Colour took a day or two to come back. My perception was off for a week. As soon as it was all back to normal, I tried again.

A woman falls in love with beauty.

The longest I ever went without my eyes was three days. I hoped maybe I would die. When I didn't, when I put them back in and could still see, I shook it forever—that itch to know if death might be better. No matter how meaningless it was, at least it was in vivid colour.

A woman falls in love with a woman.

Colour went first. I could still see everything when my eyes were in a camera—for a while—but once they were back in my head it was greyscale. It happens, from time to time, so I waited a few days, and then a few weeks, and then I realized it wasn't coming back and I disappeared for ten days. I gave away all the art in my apartment, all my furniture, painted my walls white, ordered a whole new apartment from IKEA online in white and grey and black-brown. I asked my wife to buy me grey and black sweaters, shawls, dresses. If I was seeing in greyscale, I was living in greyscale. I almost lost everything. My next films weren't black and white because of some artistic vision, although I liked that people thought so. They were in black and white because I didn't know how long my eyes would still be able to film in colour.

A woman falls in love with a life.

It was all more painful than I could ever have imagined. No fool thinks ripping their eyes out will be painless, but I suppose we are all just foolish enough.

A woman falls in love with loss.

I could use the camera for about six months after I went completely blind. Maybe it would have lasted longer if I'd been more responsible; I'll never know. I don't really care. Once I lost sight altogether and the only way to see was by filming, I filmed constantly. That *documentary*, as they ended up calling it, was for nobody except myself.

A woman falls in love with grief.

They couldn't decide how to arrest me. That's the trick: be sure to rebel naked, and they will be afraid to touch you. Forty years later and my cunts were off causing trouble again, that goddamn clip playing on the sides of buildings all over the city. Being Eva Hudson-Smith has its advantages; people will do most things for you, if you ask. And my very own cunt front and centre this time, my soft and folded body, everything I had ever been told to shut up about. Blood on my face, blood on my hands, eyes back on the bedstand, my naked ass walking blind across the Ambassador Bridge. But how do you arrest a famous, naked, blind old woman?

A woman falls in love with her past.

We are so loud. Loud and fragrant. We betray ourselves: too much cologne, not enough soap, fresh lipstick, rustling clothes, tapping feet. There is so much more to us than we would like to admit. I can hear how people's lips move when they talk. I can hear if they are talking with their hands. If they are looking at me, past me, at their phone. We are so used to this shield we have and we've never even bothered considering it a shield. But without your makeup and your hair and your clothes and your posture you are just bones and blood and muscle and it is an orchestra underneath it all. Sometimes it is an orchestra playing an entirely different symphony from the cacophony you selected that morning, week, year. Mine was.

A woman falls in love with herself.

I haven't been able to go to the movies in a long time. It is too intimate; I hate the way I cry, the way everyone else doesn't. I don't know how we are all expected to leave the theatre so cracked open like that.

A woman falls in love.

I was surprised to find out there was more to life than making movies.

A woman falls in love.

The Beginning

In which you meet a story

Finn: the heart

*T*he heat from outside had managed not only to find its way into the studio, but to intensify and revive the years of old blood and sweat that had seeped into the walls from every artist who'd ever passed through. A half-dozen oscillating fans moved the blood and sweat and heat from easel to easel, providing as much relief as the breeze from a sidewalk subway grate on an August afternoon. Sweat had collected under Stephen's sunglasses and in the small of his back, rivulets slipping over his skin and under his belt. One of the last to arrive, he hurriedly picked out a smock from the rack, gratefully pulled off his sweat-stained shirt, and pulled on the button-down smock, eyes downcast and still shaded.

"Are you okay to stay over here while Daddy works?" Stephen asked. Finn didn't seem bothered by the heat at all, already skipping toward the prop closet, swishing her tie-dyed dress around her as she went. He intercepted her, pushing his sunglasses up onto his head and kneeling down to catch her eye. "You can't play with those here, Finn. That's why we brought your art supplies, remember? How about you sit at this desk and make something we can show Mommy when she gets back, hmm?" He reached around to pull the backpack off her shoulders and set up the tiny canvas and toy organs on the desk. Finn stared lovingly at a purple feather boa heaped on the floor just outside the prop closet, smiling widely when a tall woman in a dark purple smock swept it up off the floor and held it out toward Stephen.

"Another artist in the family, Mr. O'Brien?" The feather boa cascaded out of her hand, glittering and swaying in the various fans' crossfire, complementing her smock. She joined the pair of them, bending down on one knee to hold out the boa. "I'm Deanne. What's your name?" Finn clutched her dress and swayed from side to side, looking from the boa to her father to Deanne and back again. "It's okay, you can wear this while your dad works tonight. It'll go really well with your dress." Deanne reached out to help wrap the enormous boa around Finn's small frame, which still swayed. Stephen looked at his daughter, eyes deliberate, head nodding. *What do you say?* Now swathed in sparkling purple feathers, she looked back at Deanne.

"I'm Finn," she said. "Thank you. It matches your dress, too."

"What a beautiful name. And that's very nice of you to say, but I think it looks best on you. I can't wait to see what you create tonight, Finn. And it's just about time for your dad to get to work, too." Deanne smiled and walked to the front of the room, where she started writing a numbered list on the whiteboard. The room filled with the hurried silence of a small number of people settling into uncomfortable chairs and abandoning their small talk. Stephen kissed Finn on the top of her head—Finn ignored him, already settled at the desk and focused on mixing her various shades of paint for the evening's project. He slid into the chair beside his usual easel and set his eyes on Deanne.

"Small class tonight," she said. "Honestly, I'm kind of relieved. It's a bit of a tough week, and the fewer the better. If anyone needs a refresher on blood toners or organ shaping, or if you missed last week's session on texturizing, feel free to call me over after the demo. We're going to learn to work with skin tonight. Anyone here already worked with skin? A few, alright. That's good. Guys, feel free to help out your neighbours if you see something weird going on. For the majority of us, I'd like to focus mainly on the use of skin, blood, and just one organ—keep it simple tonight, since it is new territory. If you want to challenge yourself a bit more than that, you can work with texturizing and tone. I brought some extra toners and liquefiers with me tonight that you're welcome to use, just pour some into a personal container for yourself. Sound good? You guys go ahead and get yourselves ready as per usual, and I'll come around with some extra materials. Please, even you folks who have worked with skin before, please don't start working until I give the go-ahead."

The room rustled again, stirring up the heat and the sweat as everybody resettled, unbuttoned, reached for their scalpels. Nobody looked at anything but their own hands, except for Finn, who watched her father closely. It was her first time, after weeks of begging, accompanying him to a class. Her mother was out of town—easier than calling a sitter, he'd said.

Whenever they were home, he wore high-collared or crew-neck shirts that hid the long scar that halved his torso, but sometimes when he tucked her in at night, it peeked out from under a partly unbuttoned shirt.

"What's this from?" she asked every time, pushing her palm softly against his chest. Sometimes it was freshly stitched, sometimes healing, sometimes healed.

"It's how Daddy makes art." She would look under her own pyjamas and see if anything had appeared on her chest. It never had.

"But I make art. Why don't I have one?"

"Because you have to make art for a long time before you get one." And he would look over his shoulder dramatically, back and forth between Finn and the doorway, pausing until she giggled. "Don't tell your mom, but if you keep on making your art the way you do, you'll get to learn about marks like this one sooner than you might think."

"Promise?"

"I promise."

Stephen turned his back to the corner where Finn sat, rapt. Deanne turned on the speakers at the front of the room, a rough-edged instrumental album this week. The music was loud, always loud, as loud as she could reasonably make it, considering the neighbours, but the sound of the artists preparing themselves was always louder. Lip-bitten gasps, and the horrendous sound of students splitting open—cold metal nails on a brittle fleshy chalkboard, if you were attuned to it. Overall, the sound of the room was always *wet*: hands slipping on the edges of skin, trying to get a grip on the underside of a chest to heave it apart; hearts beating sloppily out in the open, slowing in their suddenly cool surroundings, comparatively; the slap of a lung hitting the workstation, still slick with the insides of whoever it came out of; the erratic drip of the artists collecting blood in their sets of tiny stained jars, ready for mixing.

As the aural atmosphere began to dry, Deanne turned the music down and dimmed the lights, bringing everyone's attention to the projection on the whiteboard: a canvas practically drenched in crimson, but wrinkled in places, mountain ranges of either nearly black or fleshy pink staggering their way through the frame.

"You may be familiar with the work of Hélène Deschamps, a visual artist who practised in the early 80s but left us only a few short years into her career. She was the first artist to bring skin into the mix in a major way, and her early work was reviled by contemporaries and critics alike, originally decried as an affront to the integrity of art itself. Not only was she bringing skin into the mix, but she was bringing the politics of her dark skin into the sanctity of a predominately white culture." Deanne paused to slowly flip through a few more slides.

"Toward the end of her career, she had essentially abandoned the traditional use of the heart and lungs in favour of unique blood blends and an emphasis on her skin, often leaving large sections of the canvas completely blank. But you didn't come here for an art history lesson! I just wanted to show you a bit about how skin can be used in your compositions—these next few are from the first copycats, a couple of years after Deschamps died. And here you can see how the form progressed, how artists started to learn how to incorporate the inherent sloppiness, softness, of skin." In the corner, Finn went between watching the slides closely and watching her own fingers, pulling gently at her skin. Deanne walked to the far corner of the room to bring the lights back up, revealing all but two of the students also pawing thoughtfully at the skin of their arms and hands.

"Now feel free to move your chairs closer," she said after a moment. "I'm going to take a little skin off my forearm for the demo, but it can scar pretty gruesomely after a while so most people like to take from more hidden areas." She sat down at a long table at the front of the room while stools scuttled tentatively closer. A dark purple towel, matching her smock, was already laid out beside a scalpel and an empty palette. She talked the class through each motion as she first drew a light rectangle, a little smaller than the size of a playing card, in the skin near the top of her wrist. A thin line of blood appeared in the scalpel's wake. She went over one of the short edges again, pressing hard enough that the skin to either side of the incision whitened, taut, until finally splitting apart. She then deepened the incision around the corners of the rectangle that touched that same short side, along the top centimetre of the longer sides.

"You'll notice I don't cut deeply around the entire section of skin I plan to use. Some instructors might tell you differently, but I find that to be a messier, more painful way of lifting the material." Using the scalpel, she pried up a few millimetres of skin from the short edge she'd jut into, then grabbed onto the skin firmly and pulled back the same way you peel a sticker from its backing. Pulling back with one hand, she used the other to drag the blade at a narrow angle from edge to edge underneath the lifted skin. A little at a time, the strip of skin in her hand lengthened as the seeping red-and-white rectangle on her arm grew. Her face never slipped from its mask of tight-lipped concentration. The initial surface-level incisions helped keep the rectangle controlled as she cut it off flick by flick. Finally, she arrived at the bottom end of the rectangle, where she pressed the blade deeply into the final edge and pulled the skin loose with a tug. She placed the rectangle blood down on the palette and wrapped the towel around her arm.

"Okay, you guys who have worked with skin before, if you do it differently, that's okay: go ahead and do it the way you know. Everyone else, please, try it the way I showed you." She put two elastics around either end of the towel wrapped around her forearm to hold it in place, swiftly cleaning off her scalpel and putting her palette out of view. She walked over to the speakers to turn the music back up. "Given our time constraints, let's keep it to three or four pieces of skin, max, and none of them much bigger than three-by-five. As always, ask for help if you need it."

Stephen and the rest of the class shifted once more in their seats, stirring their various jars of blood to keep them from thickening, pulling their faces into contemplative frowns, running their hands along the fleshiest parts of their bodies. Finn watched closely, only half-interested in her own creation. The easels for this class, unlike for the traditional painting class, held the canvases like a tabletop, and the students now danced their fingers lightly across the blank white surface, tracing outlines of a thought or a scene or perhaps nothing at all.

Finally, one woman started to work. She placed her heart in the bottom right corner of the canvas, so close to the edge it threatened to topple, and briskly started painting dark unfiltered blood in uneven circles around the rest of the surface. Another woman was carefully preparing her palette, mixing toners and liquefiers into the little puddles of blood to create different colours and textures. Others had pulled aside their smocks and were starting to peel little rectangles of skin off the sides of their torsos. Deanne paced the room slowly, checking the students' progress, handing out extra towels. The drop sheets underneath each workstation were mercifully dark, showing neither the spill from today's projects nor the stains from last week's.

A quiet hum of conversation and inquiry gradually rose to match the volume of the music, Deanne flitting now from raised hand to raised hand, the atmosphere once again wet with the sound of blood sloshing and smearing and mixing, skin squelching into the canvas and readjusted noisily again, again, again, organs slapping into place. More advanced students started snapping out their ribs, texturizing their canvases with the various edges of the bone. After an hour of working time and with twenty minutes left in class, Deanne turned the music down to call out, "Just about time to clean up, folks. Put on your final touches, take your photographs, and then I'll show you how to stitch the skin back in place." Some of the students were already pale and sweating, and at the sound of Deanne's voice they started. They rested themselves heavily in their seats. Their chests hung open.

Deanne wandered over to where Finn sat, eyes wide and liquidy as she watched her father tidy his canvas and take out his camera. Finn smiled when Deanne knelt to look at her work.

"This is beautiful, Finn!"

"Thank you, Miss Deanne." She blushed deeply and clutched at the boa still wrapped around her shoulders. "I really liked your class tonight. I liked being able to watch everyone make their art."

"I'm glad you liked it, hon. Maybe you can join one of my classes—talk to your dad about it sometime, okay?"

"Really?" She swung the ends of the boa wildly, accidentally catching Deanne in the face as she stood up to help the students with their tidying.

"Really really," she said as she walked back to the front of the class. "I run some classes with kids not much older than you are, and you'd fit right in."

With renewed vigour, Finn jumped back into her chair to finish her work for the evening. After a few minutes, she grabbed a small Polaroid camera from her backpack and photographed the piece, shaking the picture so it would appear faster. Satisfied, she hurriedly stuffed all the materials back into her pack and set her eyes back on her father, curious to see how everything spread out on his canvas now went back where it belonged.

In a corner near the speakers, Deanne unwrapped the towel around her arm and rinsed off the patch of exposed muscle underneath. She brought thread and a needle over to her table and sat down quietly, watching the artists tidy and photograph their pieces. Satisfied with his work, Stephen carefully snapped three pictures of it before grabbing his lung from the canvas. Finn watched keenly as he thrust the organ back under his ribcage. He used a strip of beige material to hold his reattached rib in place, breathed deeply a few times, and then pulled, pushed the skin from his chest back together. The music filled the room, overpowering even the distinct crunch of breastbones sliding back into place, the hiss or rush of sharp breathing. Stephen hunched his shoulders, his torso concave, and brought a threaded needle to the base of the gash down his chest, pulled it through his pale skin. The thread stuttered as he sewed. Even when he closed his eyes, briefly, to breathe hard and shallow, needle and thread in hand, Finn herself hardly blinked.

With ten minutes left in class, Deanne started her second demo. She placed the loose rectangle of skin back onto her arm, pressing it flat, matching its pale edges to the now-pinkish edges she originally cut it from. The key, she explained, was to keep the sutures loose and spaced well apart, and allow the skin to do most of the reattaching, on its own terms. Otherwise it could morph and stretch as you stitched, leaving you with a wrinkled or mismatched patch of skin. Her face, breath, and tone never changed as she pulled the thick needle and thread through her spasming forearm. Once she had tied off the final edge, she set the needle aside and picked up a folded square of gauzy bandage, one of a dozen laid out on the table beside her. She set it on top of the newly sutured rectangle, then used butterfly bandages to fasten it tightly to her arm on each edge.

"There's enough gauze and bandages here for all of you—please make sure you don't skip this step. This will help the skin heal flat and clean, with minimal scarring. If you need a bigger piece of gauze, or more butterfly bandages, let me know." Deanne tidied her demo station, then walked from easel to easel to pass out gauze and bandages. Soon the artists were shedding their smocks, wiping down their reassembled torsos with sanitizing cloths, and easing their way back into strategically loose clothing. Bloodied smocks, towels, and drop sheets piled up in the industrial rolling laundry bin in the corner by the speakers. Unlike at the start of the class, not even a murmur materialized in the studio as workstations collapsed—no pleasantries, aside from a soft "Great class, Deanne, thanks," from time to time.

"You have a good class, Finn?" Stephen's voice was soft and raspy as he collected his daughter.

"It was the best! Can I come with you again next week? Deanne said she might even have a class I can join—do you think I could join a class, Dad?"

"I don't know, hon. Let's talk to Mom about it. Did you say thanks?" Finn nodded vigorously. Stephen nodded slowly. He slipped the small backpack over her shoulders, took her hand, and they walked together into the oppressive August evening.

Eva: the eyes

*A*t 11:30, Eva looked up from her novel. Her husband strode into the lecture hall thirty minutes late and walked to the podium. He apologized to the class, blaming a dead phone. Eva picked up her own phone and dismissed the three missed call notifications and the slew of texts she'd received from him over the last forty minutes. *Why the fuck didn't you wake me up?* She watched the shadows furrowed deeply in his face while he fiddled with the a/v system. When he finally lifted his sharp blue eyes to meet the gaze of the room, she imagined the way he would scream if she were to pluck them from their sockets. While waiting for his presentation to load, he let his eyes roam the rows of students, taking questions from hesitant hands and at last his eyes found her, rested there. She felt his voice rolling over her skin while she slid her fingers under his eyelids and pulled, felt his blood running over her knuckles, felt him yell. Felt him bleed. She lowered her eyes and opened her notebook.

After class, they walked together in silence to their usual coffee shop. He sat down at their usual table while she ordered their usual drinks, and he didn't look up from his phone when she set the cups down on the table and settled into her chair. Eyes still down, he suddenly said, "You've been a bit of a bitch lately."

She was surprised by the directness of the accusation, a name-calling he hadn't revisited since he'd started going to therapy before their engagement—before he learned how to call her a bitch without name-calling.

"What?" But he rolled his eyes and laughed. *As if you don't know what I'm talking about,* he said, but somehow he didn't say it, and she wondered if he was right.

"It's a slippery slope, is all," he said with a shrug. "You're better than that." And she agreed with him: she was better than that. She was about to ask for clarification when her phone rang. She turned it over to see who was calling, and she heard him sigh.

"It's my sister," she said, holding the screen toward him, but he rolled his eyes again, stood abruptly. *Whatever,* he didn't say, looking down at her impatiently.

"I have to go." *Me or your sister?* he didn't say, and the phone eventually stopped ringing, and he sat back down.

He looked at her expectantly. Her skin felt too small for her body, her lungs too small for air. She massaged her face into a small smile.

"I love you," she said, the words tight and painful in a hollow chest. "Sorry I didn't wake you this morning." He nodded and lifted his mug to his lips. She looked away.

*E*va and her sister drove in silence along the lake, letting bluegrass fill the space between them. Eva held her camera loosely, capturing the jostling landscape and the blinding reflection from the water. She'd had her eyes out too long, for most of the drive, but the ache was a relative comfort—a tangible pain amid the underskin crawl of dread, the tingling threat of panic. The final months of her marriage lay like sandpaper against her bones, rubbing her insides raw as they drove back toward him. In her purse, beside the divorce papers, was an envelope with the pieces of her PhD acceptance letter—a salve, a soothing reminder that she was not crazy. The trees flitted past her camera. She closed her eyes, remembered: *holy shit I got in*, with the opened letter in her hands, opened on the stairs on her way up from the mailroom, and almost no time at all to be proud because right away, his *are you really thinking of going?* as if the months of talk of her moving for her PhD had never even happened, *I got in!* and she shouldn't have flinched when he put down the book he'd been reading but she did flinch, at the sound of it, the slam of it, the rattle of the tabletop, she did flinch and she shouldn't have taken a step back when he rose from the couch but she did, *I was going to give you a fucking hug, congratulations* and *oh sorry* and the ice of his arms around her almost made her shudder. It lasted hours, days. It lasted the rest of their marriage, in slammed doors and hissed cruelties and damp apologies and ultimatums. She had gathered the rage-torn pieces of the letter in the early-late hours of a Thursday morning, of a Wednesday night, alone again with his exit ringing in her ears. She had gathered the pieces of the letter and begun to tidy, had begun again to inventory the *his* and *hers* of the apartment, each time relinquishing more and more to the *his* list until finally, that night, the only thing left on her list was her side of the closet and a small box of sentimental trinkets. It all fit easily into the trunk of a cab.

A movie played at the front of the room:

A woman sits in front of a mirror on a dark red towel. Behind her, two cameras sit on two tripods, each facing the mirror, one blinking red. The mirror is ornate, massive; it leans against a light-grey wall and reflects the scene: another light-grey wall behind the woman and the tripods. The woman looks directly into the reflection of the lens. She reaches her hands up to her face.

She places the heel of her left hand against the top of her forehead and uses two fingers to pull her left eyelid up and away from the eyeball. Her right hand gently massages the lower lid and she swivels her eye calmly in its socket, pulling the upper eyelid farther and farther up. The pink interior of the upper lid glistens in the mirror.

Once the lid is almost completely detached, the woman rolls her eye downward; her right eye closes involuntarily as it follows suit. The left iris disappears.

Her left hand braces itself as she moves her right fingers up toward the space between her eye and the eyelid. She reaches her middle finger into the newly formed gap: it disappears two knuckles deep into her eye socket and a small amount of light, watery blood spills out onto her cheekbone, onto the bridge of her nose. The muscles in her jaw harden. Her teeth grind audibly. Her breath catches violently in her abdomen. Her right eyelid flutters.

She brings her right palm in close to her face and tilts her head forward. There is a small *pop*. When she brings her hand away from her face, her eye sits in her palm, pinkish and slippery, and her left eyelid droops over the empty socket. It seeps. She places the eye beside her in a clear dish and repeats the process on her right eye. When she is finished, she feels beside herself for the dish and slowly rises to her feet. She turns away from the mirror and walks to the tripods, her eyes in one hand and the other hand extended in front of her, feeling for the camera not yet filming.

She deftly slips her eyes into the battery section of the second camera, turns off the other. There is a moment of darkness and the sound of a camera turning on. The scene returns: vivid, bright, touchable in its new crispness. She stands behind the second camera, slick pink hands at her sides. Her eye sockets seep. She stares into the reflection of the lens.

The screen at the front of the room showed Eva plucking out her eyes in gritty detail. In the audience, Eva watched herself, a lifetime ago, a shadow of herself in every way. Eva watched herself—her short, dyed hair, her sallow face, her sickly collarbones—she watched herself plucking out her eyes on the screen at the front of the room, watched her colleagues, students, and peers look on, or look away, or look at each other or their drinks. She felt someone move closer to her.

"Kind of pretentious, isn't it?" Eva didn't turn her head to look at the woman who'd spoken, but could feel her long hair brushing against her arm. She couldn't stop a crooked smile.

"Is it?" she asked, eyes still watching the screen where her movie was playing. The woman's soft body pressed into Eva's side; Eva felt the woman tilt her head in, look up at her smile, decide whether shallow criticism might build or break a bond with this particular stranger, if this particular stranger was worth it.

"I mean, the inattention to lighting and framing just seems so . . . simple. Wouldn't it be more powerful to have something so gruesome be, like, exquisitely produced?" Eva's smile cracked into a grin despite herself, and she turned toward her critic, a woman who seemed to be around her age, probably a student like her.

"Interesting consideration. What brings you here tonight?" But she already knew she wouldn't hear the answer: the woman's eyes had brightened as soon as Eva had turned to look at her, and they shone, and she shimmered, and Eva was lost in the sharp line of her jaw, the soft curve of her neck, the clattering of her bracelets every time she gestured, in how often she gestured, in the way her long hair seemed ever at risk of getting caught up in the clattering bracelets, in how somehow this woman radiated chaos but embodied grace. It was the silence of the bracelets that drew her back to the woman's expectant eyes, a question unheard and unanswered.

"I'm so sorry," and Eva lowered her head and looked back at the woman through her eyelashes, not sorry at all, "I was admiring your style and I've managed to miss everything you just said." A miniscule flush curled up the woman's cheeks, lifted the corners of her lips, scrunched the corners of her eyes. "Forgive me. Did you say your name?" and she extended her hand and ached to feel the woman's hand in hers and was embarrassed by the want, its acceleration, her fickle gut. "I'm Eva."

"Dev," she said, and her hand was even softer than Eva had imagined, and their shared grasp was firm and it lingered, and the shine in Dev's eyes steeled into a dare, or a promise, or a threat, and Eva knew her own gaze was no match for it, knew the want was written all over her face. "Nice to meet you, Eva." Their hands fell to each of their sides and Eva turned her body back toward the screen, where a new film was playing; her eyes lingered on Dev.

"Do you have something screening tonight?" Eva asked, and Dev laughed softly and shook her head, and Eva felt herself blush, rush to correct herself, but Dev's hand had reached out again to rest lightly on Eva's arm in that breathy laugh of denial, and in that breathy laugh there was nothing Eva didn't want to capture, replay, and she was again lost.

In that breathy laugh, "No, I'm no artist, just a big nerd that loves pretentious films," and in that soft touch, "Do you?" and then it was Eva's soft laugh, edged with embarrassment, a vague gesture toward the screen and the past,

"Ah, well, yes." And unsurprisingly, even embarrassment looked good on Dev.

The next morning, Dev pulled one of her legs out from under Eva's sheets and draped it over Eva's hip while Eva ran her fingers over the curve of Dev's hip. *You look like a goddess*, Eva didn't say, not yet, not even when Dev's beautiful smile spread slowly across her face, not even when her soft lips brushed against Eva's arm, not even when she shifted and the sheet slipped further off her body. *I think this is what happiness feels like*, she didn't say, not yet, not even when Dev reached up and pulled her face close for another kiss, not even when Eva's cat surprised them both by jumping up into the bed, not even as their laughter cascaded over the mess of sheets.

"I'm glad you thought my movie was pretentious," she did say, watching Dev scratch the cat's ears and thinking it was certainly too soon to fall in love with this stranger, and yet. Dev scrunched her face up and laughed.

"I'm just a computer science nerd, what do I know about film? I just knew I needed to talk to you somehow." And talk, and talk, and talk, all night over films, over drinks, over a nightcap, over pizza, into the sunrise and Eva didn't say *I could talk to you like this forever* but listened raptly and talked quickly and kissed, and kissed, and kissed. They talked about programming, about working, about misogyny, about passion projects; about Eva's thesis, the independent film circuit, the industry dramas unveiled during her time completing her master's. Dev's soft fingers drew light circles around Eva's eyes, closed her eyelids gently, as they talked about pain and wonder and value and beauty and meaning. They talked about things that shaped them but not the people, not yet, not him, but *I can already feel the way you've changed me*, Eva didn't say, not yet, but instead watched Dev—running late for class—slip out of bed into the shower, brewed two coffees and poured one into a travel mug, wrapped a muffin in a beeswax wrap, tucked her phone number into the cup sleeve. Dev's fingers rested on Eva's as she took the coffee.

"I promise to return this soon," she said.

"I'm glad. My number's in the sleeve," and with their fingers still curled around each other, Dev leaned in and Eva was struck by the domesticity of a kiss goodbye, struck by how familiar it felt, struck by how already they didn't feel like strangers anymore.

"My number's in your phone," said Dev on her way out. "Text me soon."

Grace: the artery

*G*race held her breath as she listened to her mother's light footfalls pause outside her bedroom door. Even though she was too hot under the covers, Grace didn't dare let her flashlight escape the edges of the blanket. Last time she'd pushed curfew too far, she'd been grounded from the library for two weeks, and she *had* to get back to the library. Especially now. Finally the footfalls resumed, and Grace waited until her mother had gone into her own bedroom before letting loose her shuddering held breath.

The book under the beam of the flashlight was gruesome and dark and she was in awe of it. As she devoured story after story, the feeling that she shouldn't be reading it sat like a bowling ball in the back of her mind, but she wouldn't stop: a woman kills her husband with a leg of lamb, then feeds it to the police; a cadet bets his little finger in a dangerous wager; a man has the skin off his back displayed in an art gallery. It all felt so plausible; a shiver ran through her body, and she held her pinky finger tightly. It all felt so real, but there was no way the stories here were true. These stories were neither true nor impossible, and in them she had unveiled an entire world of possibility. Lying, she discovered, was easier than she had ever imagined.

She started trying it out here and there, just to see how it fit, telling stories to people who would never bother to check: the librarian, the cashier, the cleaners. In her journals for school, she started embellishing and omitting details of her weeks, trying to change the facts of the stories so that they better matched the feelings she wanted.

At the library, the realization that she wasn't confined to the kids' shelves was like opening a door you'd always thought was locked: it felt like breaking the rules, but nobody seemed to care. She searched for more Roald Dahl, but only pulled up all the kids' books she had already read and the book of stories she had just returned. She searched for her other favourite authors, hoping one of them would take her out of the young readers' section, just to start, just a first step, just not knowing quite where to start until there, yes, a familiar name in an unfamiliar section. She found it on the YA shelf and started to browse.

When her family moved the following year and Grace had to change schools, she took what she'd learned from her books and used them to decide what kind of story she would tell her new grade seven classmates. Even this was easier than she'd imagined, keeping up home-Gracie and new Grace without question. At home she stayed quiet, studious, tidy, helpful, while at school she tried on different selves, collecting friends and followers as she braided in fabricated pasts to build a jock, a prep, a theatre kid. People usually just believe what you tell them, she decided, unhinging herself from the need to base her stories in any truth at all. At the library, she exhausted the YA shelves and moved to general literature. Early into the morning, in her new room away from prying eyes, Grace devoured lives she had never even considered. She learned new ways of being human, but she was running out of places to try them.

Even though they had hardly been in their new city for a year, she had already walked past the stationery store hundreds of times, often going out of her way to end up on the side street lined with beautiful, ivy-clad houses and the occasional home storefront. The shop window was set back from the street, difficult to linger at, but she would do her best, straining to admire the colourful notebooks, the tastefully themed stationery sets and—of course—the word processors. Today, she walked slowly up the cobblestone path to the shop entrance, drinking in the details of the window display she could never normally make out.

Inside, the store seemed to shimmer in the sunlight: small bottles and jars of toners, thinners, and dyes shone in massive, cubby-style shelves that lined one entire wall of the small space. Another large case had brushes and pencils arranged in a gradient that somehow blended both size and shade seamlessly. A floor-to-ceiling bookshelf housed hundreds of blank books, from delicate hand-stitched notebooks to imposing, leather-bound sketchbooks, and in the centre of the store, their table displays showcased bright stationery sets, specialty envelopes, and handmade stationery organizers. At the back of the store, locked in glass display cases, was what she was searching for: fountain pens and word processors.

She had found a grade twelve writing textbook at her school library, and she had convinced the librarian to let her copy the pages of the book that showed students how to use a fountain pen. She'd practised drawing her blood for the reservoir with a syringe, and though the crooks of her arms were rough and bruised, she felt ready to use a real pen. She walked up to the glass cases and peered at the different pens, eyes bouncing over the signs warning against use for children under fifteen. She stopped at a tray of metal pens coated in soft pastel colours, and a woman appeared to help her.

"Do you know what you're looking for today, sweetie?"

"I'm looking for a gift for my mom," Grace said. "She journals every weekend, and her pen is a little old. She really likes pink, maybe that one there?"

Early into the morning, in her new room away from prying eyes, Grace tried her hand at writing the stories down.

Late into the night, alone, Grace learned that bleeding was a way of being human.

The Middle

In which a story takes place

Finn: scarring

*S*he watched her heart pulse in a dark pool of congealing blood.

Shifted it slightly to the left.

On the canvas, the blood had started to dry. She tilted it at a slight angle so that the thick, brownish liquid could drip, like old cream, away from her heart.

She took one of her rinsed-off lungs from the palette and placed the shiny pink meat across the gooey streaks of blood falling from the heart.

Satisfied, she grabbed her Polaroid and photographed the piece.

She attached the photo to her artist's statement and put it on top of her growing portfolio before tending to the bandages on her chest. The blood they soaked up had started to cake; they stuck as she tried to peel them off. Finally, the bandages removed, her bare chest gaped: a searing red line, still dripping blood, vertically halved her torso. She gathered her heart and lungs. In the bathroom, she stepped into the shower and rinsed them gently before setting the organs in a custom shower caddy. After a quick body rinse she felt for the gash in her chest; she grasped at its edges and pried herself open.

The skin peeled away from her sternum like suction cups, with sounds to match. She pulled the gash apart carefully, from her clavicle to a few inches above her belly button. In the bottom of the bathtub, pink ribbons formed, swirling and chasing the clear water down the drain. The shower walls swayed around her—she had worked too long, ignored the light-headedness when it had just begun. Her shaky hands grabbed the heart from the shelf and thrust it through her ribs, which moved apart grudgingly under pressure. She pushed in her lungs as quickly as she could, then pinched her skin tightly and pulled it back over her torso before shutting off the water.

Before she'd started working, she had laid out the sewing kit on the bathroom sink beside a bottle of Tylenol. With a towel around her waist, she now popped two capsules into her mouth and reached for the needle. The thread dragged through her skin like rust: catching on something, on skin, on fat, who knows. They warn you about that, the first time you have to sew yourself back together. About how hard you have to stab the needle, about how hard you have to pull, about how it catches. She chewed the inside of her lip vigorously and every few seconds exhaled forcefully, always unaware she had ever been holding her breath. After she tied off the stitches just above her navel, she washed her hands and slipped on a soft, loose cotton dress before cleaning up. She stopped to sit at the foot of the bed, spine hunched, examining the mess. Her head was heavy, her chin drifting downwards into her chest. If she left the cleaning too long, it would dry, it would crust, it would take three times longer than if she did it now. She sighed deeply, letting her eyelids drift close on the exhale. The shallow breath in her chest lifted her chin up-down, up-down. Her head lolled to the left, her cheek catching on her shoulder before her head continued past and she jerked awake. Through heavy eyelids, she surveyed the mess once again.

She leaned back into her mattress and rolled onto her side, hugging her knees into the fetal position. So it would dry, so it would crust.

She slept.

On her desk, six photographs were arranged in a rectangle. She had been assembling her portfolio for weeks, the final make-or-break assignment of college—if you hadn't already been broken by the feedback, of course. Just a month before the semester's end, during her routine mandatory medical check-in, the health advisors had threatened to pull her out of classes. *Your activities have been too risky*, they droned. *This could be fatal if you refuse to show some caution*, and so on. But she already knew that her two years of trying to accommodate each professor's preferences had been nearly lethal. She'd spent hours poring over six semesters' worth of contradictory assignment comments to tailor a portfolio that would satisfy all of them.

72—Great work. Original idea, very well executed. Leans a bit toward shock art though—think about tidying up your lines, clip your heart a little bit. It will help for future assignments if the veins and arteries are more under control. Also the clean lung is only surface-clean. Consider shaving off irregularities so that it is smoother all around.

63—Your concept had potential, but you seem restrained in this piece. It feels like you didn't want to go big with your idea, even though it's such a big idea. The blood is very diluted and controlled, which doesn't quite fit with your description of what you're trying to convey. Skin seems like an afterthought. Overall, the execution of such a passionate concept lacks passion, in favour of craft.

58—Messy and indulgent. This piece is a huge departure from the rest of your work in this class, and while the risk was bold

the result misses the mark, the heart of the piece almost drown-
ing in the excess you've tried out here. The amount of blood
you use in this piece conveys an unwanted(?), aggressive mes-
sage. Your heart is very tailored and clean, as are your lungs,
but they are overwhelmed by the distribution of blood.

89—This is an absolutely beautiful piece of art, Finn. Your heart
is picturesque and immaculate, and the blood is toned just right.
Your lines are clean and convey a wonderful sense of control over
your message. I would recommend adjusting your lungs a little bit
for your future pieces; they are a little bit rough and unruly, unap-
pealing to the eye and unfitting for such a lovely, clean style.

94—Gruesome, passionate, great work. Lungs are a bit smooth,
and the veins and arteries from your heart are very generic;
detracts from overall honesty of the piece although the skin is
an expert touch. Consider roughing up heart and lungs.

She couldn't afford the tools to texturize her organs
again, so her perfectly tailored heart and lungs under-
mined even the most aggressive pieces. Every time she
put them back she could feel the emptiness they used to
fill. By this time, her lungs were missing nearly a quarter
of what she was born with. The veins and arteries attached
to her heart were too skinny to effectively perform; her
chest ached for days after she put it all back in, her butch-
ered muscle trying its best to push just enough blood,

just enough oxygen, just enough survival back through her body. She had learned to deprive herself of what she once thought was necessary, learned to get by on these new, mutilated organs so that her art would satisfy her audience. She had learned that what she was born with was not what would help her to succeed.

Create a 3×3-foot work that addresses one of the following statements:

"Only those who dare to fail greatly can ever achieve greatly." (Robert F. Kennedy)

"If you haven't found anything you are willing to die for, you aren't fit to live." (Martin Luther King, Jr.)

"It is better to be looked over than overlooked." (Mae West)

You have 45 minutes to complete your piece under the supervision of the panel. Be prepared to answer questions before, during, and after your exam. (90 minutes)

She didn't know any of the professors who were assigned to her panel. The timed exam would be the last component of the final assignment. Students would be graded for process, execution, how well they addressed the topic, originality, and aesthetic value.

"Please state your name for the panel," said a tired old man wearing thick-rimmed glasses and a grey three-piece suit. His deep-red tie was bright against his white shirt and dark skin, sinking into the V of his vest down the same line he would have razed with a scalpel many years prior.

"Finnegan Green."

"Place your portfolio on that table to your left, please." The woman who spoke was the youngest of the three, boldly wearing a low-cut blouse that showed the faded purple line that marked her as an artist. It was faint against her skin, diving underneath the navy-blue fabric that hid the rest of the scar. Finn placed the folder with her photographs on the table.

"You have decided which quotation you will address?" Finn nodded. The final member of the panel was a severe, silver-haired woman wearing a black, high-collared dress to hide her scar. The judges' scars were long healed, their trimmed, battered hearts beating tiredly, their breathing short and shallow. Finn wondered if they remembered how it felt: to have a heart beat comfortably, to breathe hard, to breathe deeply.

"Please begin."

She pulled out her kit, grabbed the gauze, took hold of her scalpel. The judges looked on, and she wondered if she could catch sympathy in their expressions. The old man was holding his tie; the stern woman had crossed her arms over her hidden scar; the young one pressed her hand flat against her exposed scar. The metal was cold as always, she inhaled sharply the way she always did, they all heard the familiar sound of blade splitting skin and (they remembered how it felt and) she laid herself out on the table between them, still beating, still breathing, still shivering and dripping and alive, and she couldn't quite stop the agonized, relieved moan that escaped her as she applied the gauze to the gaping, bleeding, searing red line she'd just drawn down her chest.

The room exhaled.

She focused on the canvas.

*I*n the four years since Finn had graduated from university and moved into her draughty studio loft, her mother had visited twice: once while it was still empty, to supervise Finn while she scrubbed down every available surface, and once when Finn hosted a small arts salon, six months later. Then, for three and a half years, Cleo had found every reason possible to avoid crossing her daughter's threshold.

"You can wait outside, you know," Finn called from the bathroom, imagining her mother's twisted face as she stepped into the apartment. The blood in the rugs ranged from a crispy pink to a caked-in black; the laminate flooring was speckled with dried or drying puddles of brown and crimson.

"I wish you wouldn't say that," Cleo called, but she bit back a gag imagining the bathroom tile, the shower floor, the sink. It was always so much starker against the awful white of the bathroom. In the living room, Cleo avoided looking at the workstation in the corner of the room, avoided even standing near it, the air moist and rusty and emanating outwards, rooted in the damp splatter underneath the table. A first aid kit from last Christmas lay in a corner, still sealed with plastic.

"Say what? That you have the option of being comfortable and I won't be offended?"

"I can be in your house, Finn, I helped you fix it up for goodness' sake."

"Don't use me to lie to yourself, Mom," and it was Finn's personal brand of razor-sharp, non-judgmental truth, and Cleo didn't bother trying to defend herself. Instead, she clenched her jaw and crept to the kitchen, a relative haven. Here, the floor was only barely splattered, and the counters and walls were the same clean mint green they'd picked out when Finn first moved in after graduating. The same colour the rugs used to be, the throws, the duvet. Cleo had been so ready, then, to be better: reliable, supportive, helpful. A mother like Finn's father. *Red or black, maybe purple*, Finn had kept saying as they'd trudged through Bed Bath & Beyond. And of course Cleo insisted otherwise: *this colour is so classic, you won't regret it.*

She stared at the clean walls of the kitchen and pulled her hands over her face. She breathed in, relishing the lingering scent of hand sanitizer. She pulled open the fridge and cringed at all her Tupperware containers, grey and fuzzy, among dozens of bottles and cans—empty, full, flat—of Perrier. She took one and poured it into a cracked mint-tinted glass. She stood over the sink and sipped from it as it dripped.

"They come in a container already, genius." Cleo started and turned to the empty doorframe where Finn stood smiling and pulling her hair into a loose braid. "You don't need to pour it into a leaky cup."

"Most people, I think, wouldn't bother keeping a leaky cup."

"Right." Finn tied off the braid and stepped toward her mother, reaching out to take the cup. She dumped the contents in the sink, slid open the screenless window above it, and tossed the cup out. It landed out of view in a rustle of plastic. She got a half-full can from the fridge and sipped from it, then reached in for another can and held it out to her mother. Cleo took it and stared out the window. She felt her resolve folding into itself like a dirty napkin.

"What's the point in dressing up if you aren't going to cover that up?" she snapped suddenly, waving her hands at Finn's exposed scar, raw and leaking and swollen, half-heartedly sutured and secured with a few butterfly bandages and a small amount of gauze. Finn squinted at her mother and loosely furrowed her brow. Her mother shook her head. "Forget it, we're late," she said, unnecessarily smoothing her own dress. "I have some Tide to Go in the glove compartment if you end up needing it."

In the car, Finn stared pointedly out the passenger-side window. She could feel her mother glance over every few minutes, could hear the occasional shift in her breathing when she was thinking of starting a conversation. Finally,

"Do you remember the first time?"

"What?"

"The first time you took your lungs out. Do you remember? You got that boy, the neighbour's son..." Finn smiled out the window, small enough that her mother wasn't likely to see.

"Anders, yeah. I remember you just about killing us afterwards, that's what I remember."

But that wasn't true, not entirely. That first time, she'd convinced the perpetually nervous Anders to help her under threat of death. *If you don't help me with this, I might die*, she'd told him after school one day. It was a year after she'd convinced her mother to let her start art classes; it was days after her father's diagnosis. Her own death meant nothing to her, not then, not in the shadow of her father's illness. But it meant something to Anders.

That first time, they'd laid down a double layer of red dollar store towels underneath her, and he sat frozen beside her with more as she opened her laptop and started the video. *No painkillers, they make you bleed more* she'd said as he begged her to do something that would make it easier. *Easier for who?* she had muttered, turning her eyes back to the screen, to the scalpel, to the dotted line going from the middle of her sternum down her chest nearly to her belly button. *It's going to bleed a lot the first time you do it*, every tutorial, textbook, and teacher warned them. She had bribed an older art student to buy her the tonic—the "virgin tonic," they called it. To slow it all down, that first time.

She had smeared the tonic onto her torso, dried her hand, picked up the scalpel and clicked play. The video had played quietly, Anders sweating and looking at the ceiling, and she bit down hard on a clean sock and raked the blade along the line. Towel after towel from Anders had filled with blood while she pried the skin open and reached under her ribs, her lung slippery and hot in her fingers. She could feel the towels shaking as she took them. Finally, she had spat the sock out of her mouth. *Well, that wasn't so bad.*

He had looked back at her then, pulling his gaze down the wall and across the floor. It caught on the red towels—redder, damper—on a slash of pink amid the mess. Her lung glistened outside of her body. His tinny whine had echoed in her bedroom, grown into a wavering scream—*shut up!!*—before he'd fainted.

Her mother had never forgiven them after that, after her father had barged through the door onto the scene. The towels had done their job well: though soaked, the scene wasn't gruesome, and it had taken him a moment to piece it all together. Finn had been calmly stitching her chest with a care she would lose rapidly as the years passed. Her stitches were still tight then, her bandages clean and deliberate. *Everybody is fine, Dad*, she was saying as she'd prodded Anders awake. Her father had this look for her, for these moments: a smile hidden in his beard while his eyebrows bushed down over narrowed eyes. *Oh my Finnegan...*

"You never really trusted him after that, even when he helped us out while Dad was sick," Finn said scornfully, despite herself. She switched the radio to CBC and stared out the window and she grabbed a tissue from the car door to hold it against a seeping part of her chest. Her mother tensed and focused her eyes on the bumper in front of them.

"His mother hated us for it, I was trying to appease her," but the lie was clunky and obvious to both of them, and she could feel Finn's eyes rolling just out of view. Finn shook her head and rubbed her face like her father used to rub his short, trimmed beard. Finn, always the cause of that exasperated rubbing, would say to him *You'll rub it right off someday soon, Dad*. In the car, Cleo and Finn both felt the years-old fight come and go between them: that Cleo never wanted art in the house to begin with, that Finn had just wanted someone to blame for her father's death, that Cleo would still do anything to stop her from making art, that Finn was still looking for a person to hold all of her fears and failures. The truth jagged and opaque amid the noise. They ran their lines silently.

"Right," said Finn finally, and Cleo sighed, and it was over. It was over when Finn said it was over. She always had to have the last word. She had even fought for an open-casket funeral, and Cleo had found out later it was so she could slip the most hated family photograph into the coffin. *The shaving incident*, they called it. Their lives just a series of "Finn-cidents," from the diagnosis until the end. They'd never fixed the bathroom lock after her father had broken in to find her and Anders, ever the dedicated sidekick, shaving her head. *Join the party, Dad!* she yelled, somehow even louder than he was yelling, and suddenly laughter was echoing off the tiles. Tears folding into the creases on his face, seeping into his beard. His smile warped while his eyebrows bushed down over narrowing eyes—eyes already sunken, hair already thinning from the radiation, fifteen-year-old Finn joyfully waving the buzzers inches from his nose. *Oh my Finnegan . . .* He finished the job, added his beard to the mess on the floor, added what was left of his hair. *Cleo, come here! We need a picture! The beginning of the end, Cleo—*

Finn pulled down the sun visor to look at herself in the mirror as they pulled into the parking garage. Her chest had stopped seeping, but not before staining a small area of her new dress. Cleo gestured at the stain remover between them, but Finn ignored her. Still, Cleo slipped it into her pocket when Finn turned away to step out of the car.

"Finn, wait," she called. The sound of her own voice caught her off guard. Wait for what? And she almost didn't, a little hitch in her step and a few more before she stopped. Cleo watched her daughter pat her pockets, see if she'd forgotten something. Watched her turn back, a skeptical frown wrinkled loosely between her eyebrows, Stephen's eyes searing through the distance. Cleo's breath caught.

"Thank you. For inviting me to this."

"You *are* my mom, Mom. I wouldn't be an artist without you, as much as you hate to hear it." Cleo's hand rose involuntarily to her throat. "We're going to be late." Finn shook her head and continued through the parkade, down the stairs and onto the street, oblivious or impervious to the disgusted stares from passersby at the damp brown bandages on her chest. Cleo trailed at a distance and wished she were a different kind of mother, wondered if she had ever been a different kind of mother. She thought about that perilously thin line between fear and anger—thin and constantly moving, so often not a line at all—about every time she'd walked past an open studio door and wondered if the body behind it was sleeping or unconscious, if it was an emergency or an overreaction. She wondered if other mothers had different daughters, or if it was normal, the incessant fear of everything on behalf of someone who never seemed to be even remotely afraid. As they walked, she felt her usual owed apologies begin to pile up—every time more to pile, stuffing themselves down her throat, crowding into her lungs, her stomach, her heavy legs, her stomping feet. Waiting for someone to pull them out, the ultimate trick, an endless coloured scarf pulling and pulling and pulling and pulling and.

Finn made no effort to slow down or look back, not at corners, not at lights, not at the door, and Cleo had to jog to catch up. She remembered the year after Stephen died, when Finn had transferred high schools after being suspended for fighting. She'd started at the new school with a broken nose and a black eye. *Aren't you embarrassed?* Cleo had asked, but of course she hadn't been. She'd spent that whole year—and every year since—chasing Finn, always late, always trying to be a different kind of mother, a mother in charge, a mother with something to offer, a mother like Stephen.

She caught up to her daughter at the elevator, where the other occupants looked away from her damp, rusty sternum that seemed to fill the whole space.

Aren't you embarrassed?

A staple question from mother to daughter at any given moment: standing up for seconds at a buffet; spending the day in a coffee-stained blouse; showing up early; showing up late; showing up underdressed; bleeding on someone's furniture.

Why should I be?

When the elevator opened, Finn extended her arm to hold open the doors. *Aren't you embarrassed?* The hostess greeted the elevator occupants and collected their names, provided them with their passes. When Finn approached, the hostess smiled and pulled out two more passes.

"Welcome to the Sobey Art Award gala, Ms. Green, let me show you and your mother to your seats."

Why should I be?

After the Sobey Award, all the galleries Finn had been querying for months started responding to her emails. The first time she was approached by a reproduction factory, she scoffed and turned it down; she was a gallery artist, not a mall artist. The first time she was approached by an agent, he told her she wouldn't have to keep the barista job she'd been holding on to since high school. It wasn't the whole truth, but just before her thirtieth birthday, she finally handed in her notice. When her agent asked if she wanted to take a tour of the factory that was reproducing her latest piece, she responded quickly—*no, god no, please no*. But as she saw her art in more and more places, as her scar faded, her curiosity got the better of her. What did it look like, to make art without cutting someone open?

Rows of canvases hung from the ceiling, each with her blood and guts recreated to perfection. All throughout the factory, employees were handling her reproduced art, getting her blood all over their hands and aprons. Black aprons over white dress shirts, on men and women alike. Impractical, surely? One employee seemed to be tasked with disassembling the flawed canvases: Finn watched the person pulling her heart, her lung, a swatch of skin off the canvas and throwing them in a metal bin to their left, stacking the bloodied canvas in a plastic one to their right. Despite their rolled-up sleeves, blood slipped up to their elbows in slow-moving streaks and seeped into the white fabric, decorating more and more of the shirt. Finn watched the metal bin fill with faulty organs, watched the white shirt turn pink, turn brown.

"Are you okay?"

Finn's eyelids fluttered dangerously. Just as she looked away, another employee approached to replace the bins, completely filled with discarded organs, with empty ones.

"Hey, do you guys have some water around here?" she heard her agent whispering to the guides. How many woozy artists he must accompany through this warehouse, just as he accompanied her to their clinic when they needed her blood, heart, and lung samples to start the mass reproduction. How much false concern he must have to carry with him each day for moments like these.

"Finn, you look like you've seen a ghost. I have a few details to clear up, but you can wait outside," her agent said to her kindly.

"Thanks," she said. *Like she'd seen a ghost.*

So they asked her to leave, and she left through the wrong door.

Piles of dripping dress shirts oozed in the corners of the room, and her feet slipped around underneath her. She reached back to catch the door before it closed, but there was no handle and instead she slammed it shut. Her eyes adjusted as she inched forward: small doors, like garbage chutes about two feet across, lined the walls. Spaced only an inch apart, single metal handles in the middle of each square glowed like embers in the low, hazy lighting. When she finally reached the large door on the other side of the room, a beacon beneath the exit sign, it opened and fluorescence bled into the chamber. But curiosity won: before she left, she reached out and pulled open the nearest of the small square doors, her hand slipping wetly on the handle—a laundry chute, packed with more once-white shirts, a soft *drip drip drip* echoing up from beneath them.

The small door clanged shut, and the purgatory seared in a wedge of light as she scampered into the next room.

The next room was too bright, and she squinted at the new surroundings: black tiles, white grout stained brown, silhouettes of showerheads lining black-tiled walls. The room was long and narrow, the floor still slippery under her feet, the soft *drip drip drip* still echoing out of tiny drains scattered around the room, the soft *drip drip hummm* blending into the lights, into the fan, the air thick with steam and bleach and old blood. A sink and a soap dispenser glimmered beside each showerhead. The soap was foamy, sickeningly white against her palm, red-brown with blood from the handle. She watched the soap, the water, the blood, watched it run down the drain, wondered whose art she was washing away.

At the end of the room, rows of plush red towels hung from wall to wall, floor to ceiling. She dried her hands and cautiously exited through the next door.

More laundry chutes welcomed her into a sterile change room. Beyond them, clean shirts glared white under the rows and rows of fluorescent lighting, starkly different from the piles of sodden shirts she had left behind. A stack of black drawers sat beside each closet, and wide full-length mirrors were installed around the room. She pulled open a drawer to reveal piles of neatly folded slacks, sorted by size. It slid closed when she let go to turn toward one of the mirrors. Despite everyone's best efforts, a spot of blood had dried into her collar.

She scratched at the spot with a nail-bitten finger and she looked at herself. A soft, beige silk blouse tucked into a pencil skirt. *Is there something specific I should wear?* she had asked her agent earlier in the week. *Whatever makes you feel comfortable, Finn.* Hair pulled into a tight bun, buttons done up right to her collarbones. Just another young professional. *Comfortable like physically, or like I fit in?* she'd tried to clarify. *Just wear whatever you want that morning, I'm sure nobody will notice.* The spot of blood had turned into a small dried firework on her collar, brown chalk on a silken sidewalk after the rain. She frowned at her reflection. A murmur of conversation fell into the buzzing room from under the door she hadn't reached yet. Startled, she untucked her blouse and quickly pulled it over her head, stuffing it into her purse. She grabbed a stiff white shirt from the closet in front of her and slipped it over her shoulders, buttoning it from the top down, leaving it hanging over the decorative waist of her skirt.

She waited with her head close to the final door until the murmur of conversation faded, then pulled open the door to find herself in an empty break room. She crossed one more room, opened one more door, and found herself in the lobby of the factory, where they had begun their tour. Just as she lowered herself into an armchair, she heard her agent laughing his way toward her. The laughter stopped a safe distance away; abruptly, a careful silence built back up into jovial conversation. Her agent and their guide from the warehouse finally walked around the corner, and she stood up to meet them in the middle of the room.

"It was great to meet you, Finn," said the warehouse employee who had led their tour. "We hope you're confident in our ability to handle your work with the care as we move forward." Finn shook the thick hand extended toward her, forcing her strongest grasp.

"Great to meet you too. Thank you for the tour." She smiled as graciously as she could. "Sorry to leave early—this weather really gets into my head sometimes."

"Not a problem, of course."

Her agent placed the tips of his fingers on her shoulder and beamed at the whole group.

"Well, gentlemen, we'd best let you get back to work. What was the name of that bar you mentioned again? I'll join you there sometime soon. Always a pleasure, of course. Thank you for another spectacular tour and efficient business meeting. You guys—you're the best meetings I get every month."

In the car, her agent didn't say much after ascertaining she was feeling better, and no thank you she didn't need an Advil, and yes, just home thank you. He had pulled out his phone almost as soon as they'd left the warehouse, now absorbed in it entirely.

"Whereabouts is home?" asked the driver through the rear-view mirror.

"Liberty Village, thank you." Finn glanced sideways at her agent. "So, is there—do I have to do anything else, now?"

"Hmm?"

"What do I have to do now?"

"Nothing, Finn. Just leave it to me."

Half an hour and another awkward goodbye later, Finn fielded the stares in the elevator as her fellow young professionals eyed her starchy new shirt hanging horribly over the waistband of her skirt. Nobody at the warehouse had noticed, it seemed—not even her agent—noticed that she'd changed, noticed that she'd stolen a shirt. A white blouse is a beige blouse is a silk blouse; an artist just a person covered in blood.

Outside her door leaned a large thin box—art, otherwise the doorman would have kept it downstairs. She pushed it into her living room: shades of light grey and white lit up with garish throws and pillows. (Impractical, surely.) She took off her skirt and draped it over a grey armchair, unbuttoned her new shirt, took a closer look at the box, pulled out an envelope tucked into the top.

Inside, a note:

Ms. Green,

   Our sincere apologies in the delay returning your piece to you. Your lungs proved quite the feat to reproduce! Your work is so unique and original, and we couldn't bear to misplace even one tiny detail. We're so grateful for the opportunity to work with you on this piece, and we hope the process is going smoothly for you. Please let us know if we can assist you in any way.

She sighed. She crossed the room with the barely opened box under her arm and unlocked a door beside the kitchen. Without bothering to turn on the light, she slid the box into the room. Fingers dancing lightly across her scar, Finn stared into the darkness at her unfinished projects before closing and locking the door. She examined her hands for blood, but of course there wasn't any. Long-dried blood won't get on, or come out of, anything.

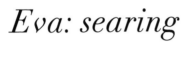

Eva: searing

*T*he room had darkened around her, a pink sunset glow come and gone through the bay window, and the computer screen illuminated Eva's furrowed face with an eerie light, flashing as she watched video after video of different artistic processes on YouTube. Her eyes watered. She started when Dev tapped lightly on the door frame behind her, grimaced as she straightened in her chair and spun around.

"Mind if I turn on a light?" Dev asked, not waiting for an answer to do so. "How's it going?" she asked. Eva shrugged, shook her head.

"Endless," she responded. "Endless and bloody." Dev murmured inarticulately, her sound that meant *of course* or *so it goes* or *as we do*, that way she had of not dismissing a grumpy mood but also not giving it any more importance than it needed. In the inarticulate murmur, Eva could feel Dev's soft palm on her cheek, could feel a soft curling around her heart, an unclenching in her jaw, a reminder. She breathed in and felt the air fill her body, felt it for the first time all day. "Have you eaten yet?" Dev shook her head. "Can I talk it over with you at dinner?"

"Always."

In the two years since they'd met, Eva had delved into her PhD research and begun work on her second short film. Her divorce had been finalized, and she and Dev had gone to the most expensive cocktail bar they could find to celebrate. Dev had finished her master's, and together they had found a small apartment not far from the university. Dev proposed; Eva said yes. Somehow, Eva had fallen into a domestic bliss she had never believed in, blissful since that first kiss goodbye, blissful in every morning she woke up to Dev's body beside her in bed, a contentment irreconcilable with the constant ache behind her eyes, and yet reconciled nonetheless in every quiet moment, soft glance, small touch.

Dev poured their drinks and set the table while Eva warmed their leftovers on the stove and talked. *I want it to hurt the way it hurts to be alive*, she didn't say, mulling over how she wanted to string it all together. "I want it to mean something," she did say, and Dev nodded like *it will*, but it wasn't quite what she meant, so she tried again: "I want it to have meaning?" and Dev stopped nodding, tilted her head, and Eva kept trying: "I want it to be about more than the blood."

The film was going to be gruesome, an extension of her first, showing dozens of artists executing the most painful parts of their creations. She had already selected and interviewed the subjects, and she had already written the short script for her voiceover, but the visuals stayed just out of reach. She'd been watching process videos for weeks, waiting for something to settle into place, but all they did was fill her brain like the worst Tetris board she'd ever seen. She tried one more time: "I want them to *feel* it when they're watching," and Dev walked over to her to place a gentle hand on her sternum, light and warm—*they will*.

Over dinner, they picked through the voice over script together:

Do you think people realize it hurts? Hurts everyone: hurts us, hurts the people who love us, hurts the people we love. Do you think they could stomach loving the person behind the canvas? Loving someone more than you have ever loved anything, living every day just waiting for them to die?

We hear the whispers of our parents, of our mentors, of our teachers: they want us to be better. Better, they say, better than this, than everyone; than them. But also they want us to grow old. Do you ever have trouble? *They ask each other.* Do you ever have trouble making them understand you're proud?

Would you still go to galleries if you had to listen to every chest being sliced open? Would you still want it if you knew how much it hurts? If you had to clean up the blood to the soundtrack of every held breath, of every groan?

But you don't even want to see the scars.

"*D*ev, I'm so sorry—" and at the sound of Eva's voice, Dev turned sharply, and Eva cut herself short while she watched her wife's breath stutter in her chest, watched her cool eyes soften and crease with worry, watched her shoulders fall. Eva closed the distance between them with a few long strides, pulled the weight of Dev's composure into her, wound her fingers into the hair at the base of her neck. *I'm so sorry*, she didn't whisper into the soft brush of her wife's shampoo, but, "I'm here," and she kissed the top of her head, pressed their foreheads together. She slipped her arm around Dev's waist and guided her to the waiting room chairs. They sat down together, entwined awkwardly around the armrest between the seats, and Dev's hands trembled on her knees. Finally, she exhaled deliberately through pursed lips, and she looked at Eva.

"Thank you for coming," she said, and Eva felt her entire body split open from the guilt of it, from the implication that she might *not* have come to the hospital after listening to Dev's shaky voicemail, that the consequences of her own artistic crisis were that her wife of ten years could not be certain that she would care enough about her father-in-law's heart attack to table her tantrum and show up. Now, though, was not the time to apologize, not the time to defend herself, not the time to say *I have lost the ability to see colour but I have not lost my humanity entirely*, so she held Dev's face gently, instead.

"Of course," she breathed, and "What do you need, my love?" and not *I'm sorry for running away* or *I'm sorry for replacing all of our furniture* or *I'm sorry I stole the colour from your life* or *I know you will always be the colour in mine*. She didn't know when she had wandered away from that certainty, when the gentle warmth of Dev's touch stopped being the only anchor, when she had come unmoored from herself, and here with her wife's soft skin against her palm she felt herself clawing it back, the line between them, felt her throat aching with apology, felt her chest crack to consume everything she had forgotten to be grateful for. Pressed her lips against Dev's forehead, "What do you need?"

"Will you go find my mom?" Dev's voice was muffled in Eva's collar. "She went to get coffee. I think she might have gotten lost." And the truthful answer was *please don't make me leave you again* but she did leave, hurried through the labyrinthine halls, double-taking every neat silver French twist until finally she spotted the right one wandering through the gift shop. She stopped outside the entrance and watched.

The gift shop was achingly strategic—non-fluorescent lighting, non-uniformed staff, dark hardwood floors, deep armchairs around a gas fireplace. Nothing cheap, nothing harsh, nothing dead. A little portal into something distinctly non-hospital. Her mother-in-law walked slowly through the relative oasis and stared vacantly at the bland, inoffensive wares. She would occasionally pick something up to look at it more closely, but invariably placed it back on the shelf and continued her circuit, carrying a haunt along with her, her right arm clasping her left tightly, just above the elbow, and her chest sank deeper into itself with every slow breath out. The haunt filled the hollow between her collarbones and spilled down over the concavity, crept up her neck into her slack jaw and molasses blinks. Eva closed her eyes and tried to see Dev, tried to see if she had missed that haunt clinging to her wife's familiar edges, winced at how much she had missed.

When Eva returned to the waiting room with coffee and her mother-in-law, Dev's father had been admitted. They found Dev in his room two floors up, where his sleeping face looked pinched and pale. Eva laced her fingers through Dev's and squeezed. Nobody said *it's all going to be okay*.

Drying dishes beside her, Eva glanced at Dev's tired face and felt all the same apologies bubbling in her throat again. They had been staying with Dev's mother for nearly three weeks, awaiting her father's return home, which was now imminent. The urgency which had been needling her since Dev's first voicemail had finally ebbed, and the greys of her in-laws' home—a home which she knew to be filled with life and colour, hideously and brilliantly alive—had been burrowing under her skin and she itched with the pain of it, with knowing the pain was nothing, with not scratching the itch. When the dishes were finished, Dev started a pot of coffee, and Eva stood behind her, slid her hands around her waist, bent her face into the curve of her wife's neck.

"Can we talk?" she murmured, and Dev did not turn but nodded, did not return the embrace but melted into it in a tiny concession, a shy yearning. They stood together quietly, watched the coffee drip slowly into the carafe, delivered a mug and a gentle hug to Dev's mother at the kitchen table, and carried their own mugs upstairs to the guest room. They settled into the bed together, and Eva felt the weight of the last month sloughing off her skin in anticipation of a real conversation, felt a welling behind her eyes, felt her skeleton creaking underneath it all. She looked into Dev's eyes—a shimmering, rich brown until the morning, a few months ago, when Eva had woken up in black and white; now, shining black irises and gleaming whites set in soft grey skin, creases beginning to form at the corners of her eyes, sunken shadows at her cheekbones.

"I'm sorry for everything," Eva finally said out loud, and Dev shook her head like *it doesn't matter*. "I know it doesn't feel like it matters now, and it doesn't, but you didn't deserve that. You need to know you didn't deserve that. You offered to help me in so many ways and I shouldn't have left like that." She could feel more of it straining against her clenched jaw, but she held her teeth together and rested a soft gaze on her wife's slumping shoulders, on the way her knuckles whitened around her mug. A self-loathing tightened itself around Eva's muscles, pulling her body into itself, telling her to become as unobtrusive as possible, but she had been pulling and pulling and look what she had undone. She shuffled closer to Dev on the bed, reached a shaking hand out to lay heavily on her wife's thigh, and in that touch felt a bridge stretch over the valley she had dug between them. Eva, always digging valleys; Dev, always building bridges.

I love you, she didn't say, and for the first time in three weeks, her wife curled into her and shook with quiet sobs.

While Dev cried into Eva's chest, Eva held her close and tight and warm and she ran through her monologue in full: *I got lost*, she didn't say. *You made it possible for me to make the most painful work I ever wanted to make and people loved it because you loved me and I got lost in it. I'm sorry you have spent so much time building bridges. I'm sorry you have spent so much time retrieving me from the deepest part of the maze. I'm sorry that you gave me the world and all I did was get lost in it. I was so angry—I am so angry—that I only got thirty-seven years with these eyes. I'm sorry that when I lost the only thing you didn't give me, I blamed you for it. I'm sorry it has taken me so long to realize that everything you gave me was already mine to discover, and we found it together. I'm sorry I made you feel alone in this. I'm sorry I failed you.*

Dev's breath evened, quieted. She rested against Eva.

"I'm sorry I got lost," Eva said into the top of Dev's head. Dev raised her head to look at her.

"Are you back?"

"I'm back."

Dev nodded and rested her head back down on Eva's chest. Eva kissed her hair.

"Will you go to the goddamn ophthalmologist?" Dev said, and Eva laughed, and Dev laughed, and it didn't even matter that Eva couldn't tell if Dev was wearing her blue sweatpants or her grey sweatpants, because they were laughing, and Dev's laugh would always be prismatic and shimmering.

"I'll go to the goddamn ophthalmologist," she said.

"Do you still want to go to the cottage next weekend?" Dev asked, and Eva sighed, because their trips to the cottage with her film friends had always been a highlight of their summers, and she had cancelled on every single one since she'd lost colour. This would be the last one of the season, and she missed them, but she still hadn't told anyone other than Dev about her eyes. "We don't have to," Dev said after a moment. "You and I can go up alone later in the fall." There was something in her face, though, a pleading she would never voice—a need to be away, to be someone else for a moment. A woman without a sick father, without a colour-blind wife, a woman with dogs and friends and food.

"No," Eva said. "Let's go."

"Do *you* want to? What about—?" But Dev looked almost hopeful, like she needed to leave but couldn't say so. "Yes," Eva said. "Let's go."

Away from the city, the stars shone bright and countless in the sky, and in moments of silence the circle of friends around the fire would each turn their eyes upwards, drinking in the relief of being small, of being away. The fire burned hot and wild in the sharp breeze, spitting sparks from a new crackling log Eva had just thrown in.

She zipped her windbreaker closed and basked in the heat, almost uncomfortable against her face. The wind changed suddenly and the smoke made her eyes water. She pressed her hands into the hot flesh of her cheeks and looked at how the flames licked the new log, how they danced against the wind.

"What do you think, Eva?"

"Hmm?" She moved her head toward her friends without looking away from the fire, hoping they would carry on without her.

"The festival circuit—nothing really caught our eye this year. What about you?" She sighed, rubbed her eyes. She stepped back and sat on the log, rested her head lightly against her wife's shoulder.

"I suppose it depends on what you were looking for," she said finally. "I've been a bit disconnected lately, but it seems like a lot of new directors are out there this year." Dev leaned her head on top of Eva's in a tiny hug as their friends took up the conversation without her again. She stared into the fire. She imagined what it would look like to set her eyes among the coals. With her head against her wife's shoulder, she watched them burn and let her eyelids drift closed.

At four o'clock, after hours of listening to Dev's heavy sleep sighs, Eva rolled out of bed, put on her new glasses, and quietly took her laptop out of their room. She slipped past the closed doors of the other rooms of the cottage and into the living room, where she plugged headphones in and opened her computer to where she'd left off working on the latest edits. Editing the black-and-white footage felt like a throwback to her undergrad, and it was taking months longer than she would normally spend on such a short project. The greys swam together, the lighting never quite right, her cuts were too sharp, her shots were too long—nothing fit with itself, and watching and rewatching felt like pushing needles into her eyes, her useless eyes, felt like watching herself pluck her eyes out for nothing. There were no vivid colours, there was no shining clarity, there was only grey. She minimized her windows and rested her useless eyes on her desktop background, drank in the shapes, closed her eyes and saw it: her and Dev, ten years younger, on their wedding day, laughing in an Atlantic wind that whipped violently through their dresses, carried the beautiful fabric into the ocean, rippling with white-caps and iceberg blues and afternoon orange. Dev's deep-purple lipstick outlined her laugh, her dark, almost-black hair whirling around the crinkles at the corner of her shining brown eyes, her stark white dress gleaming in the late sun. Eva let her mind's eye get lost in the soft hues of the memory, in their rich, dark bouquets, in the warm lighting of their reception, in the brilliant colours of their guests' dresses, ties, shirts. She stayed there until the scene left her, and then she stayed in the darkness under her eyelids. She leaned her cheek into Dev's invisible hand and breathed deeply. She returned to her work.

Eva tiptoed to the cabin's kitchen to make a cup of tea, and the dogs circled her expectantly. She propped open the back door for them. She made her tea in a travel mug and shrugged quietly into her flannel coat to follow the dogs out into the trails behind the property. The trees were full, rustling, and the greys in front of her blended with the greens and browns of her memory. She had begun noting the shapes of the leaves, identifying differences she had never considered before—a consolation prize, she decided. After a half hour, she stopped at a modest lookout and stared out at the blinding surface of the lake. She wondered how far she could throw her eyes, if they would plummet heavily into the rocks or if they might be carried by the wind, even for a moment.

She whistled for the dogs and turned back toward the cabin, her stomach already growling for Dev's famous farewell brunch.

After eating, the group cleared the table and set to washing the dishes, putting away the food for the drive home, cleaning the kitchen, heading up to their rooms to stuff their few belongings into a duffle bag, a backpack, a tote bag. Took the dogs for a last short walk, a last long breath of the trees, of the lake, of the impending storm.

Piled everything and themselves into the car, *if we leave soon we might be able to beat the weather.*

The drive to the city would go the way it always did: they would dial themselves up to city speed, practise on each other, talking shit and spewing vitriol under the guise of passion. It would go the way it always did: Eva would win, would deflect the burning need to win by reminding whoever had accused her of winning that *opinions aren't a competition.* Dev would drive just above the speed limit and periodically turn the volume of the radio up to silence the noise, they would laugh, listen to the static and the beat, they would be silent.

At a rest stop, the whole group posed for a group picture, their last weekend getaway of the season, and Eva looked at them—revving themselves up, their kindnesses and their sharp smiles and their tender grasps, gestures— and she ducked into the car early. She pulled out her camcorder and a face cloth, clenched her jaw while she popped out her right eye and slipped it into the battery section of the camera, swiped at the mess dripping from the socket. From a distance, she watched them again, textured and shaky, on their way back to the car. They saw her, waved, protested—

"What are you doing—"

"No cameras, you *made* the rules—"

"I know, I know, it's just for me, I just love you guys."

Their bodies crushed into her, and she closed her eye and lowered the lens, shuffled into her seat with a gritty view of their feet, the dust, the asphalt. Back in her seat, she lifted the camera and pointed it out the windshield, twisted briefly to Dev turning the key and pulling out of the rest stop.

"I just love you."

"*B*aby, will you *please* stop filming for a second?" Dev was driving them to the bakery to pick up the cake for Eva's fortieth birthday party, her flannel buttons mismatched, her ponytail mostly flyaways. Ever the rock in their marriage day-to-day, Dev had never been good under pressure, but Eva had always thought it was cute. She smiled.

"You know I won't. What do you need?" Dev turned the corners of her mouth down in a cartoonish frown. In truth, Eva knew she should take a break, but she didn't want to miss a moment of this, her adorably frazzled wife pulling together the final touches of the event: the way the corners of Dev's eyes smiled upwards at the same time her scowl curled downwards; the way she kept glancing over at Eva to make sure she seemed to be having a good time;

the excited worry that plastered itself all over her beautiful face. Without colour, Eva had learned to read shadows and movement with more depth than she'd ever considered—she had watched an entirely new layer of her life unbury itself, and its details astonished her. And now she was losing even that. With her eyes in her head, Eva could only see shadows, the vaguest outlines of the world around her. With the camera, at least, she still had a colourless world in crisp detail. It ached to be filming so much, but she didn't want to lose it all without something to hold on to. *I promise I won't get lost again*, she never said, over and over again to her sleeping wife, to their dogs, to her own outline in the mirror. *I promise I won't get lost again*, but she could not promise even an inch more, and so she ached, she filmed, she annoyed her rock, they found a temporary balance.

"All I need is you," Dev said at last as she pulled into the plaza parking lot. "Do you want to come in with me?" Eva grabbed her sunglasses from the visor and slipped them over her empty eye sockets.

"Of course," she said, and Dev walked around the front of the Jeep to open Eva's passenger-side door, helped her and her camera down, glared playfully at the lens. Eva turned the camera toward the bakery storefront, its sign somewhere on the verge between tacky and coming back into style, the letters in what she knew to be a dirty, faded pink. Inside, Polaroids and framed pictures covered every inch of wall space, of weddings and engagements, of children's birthday parties, of anniversaries and baptisms. A short man with coiffed silver hair emerged from the back of the store in a clean apron and threw his arms open.

"Devon! Eva! Ah, *buon compleanno, principessa!*" He pulled each of them into a bear hug, kissed each of their cheeks. "Let me go get your cake, I promise I've outdone myself again." And when he re-emerged, Eva nearly gasped: the two-tiered cake was dynamic and alive, with flowers drawn up along the sides and piled extravagantly atop the second layer. She could tell from the shades of grey that the colours were vibrant and full, and she walked slowly around the table with her camera, waiting for the layers to unbury themselves.

"Tell me," Eva said quietly, and Dev slid an arm around her waist and began speaking softly.

"It's perfect," and Eva nodded because yes, she could already see that. "The background is mostly this unbelievable plum colour, it's so dark and rich, and those highlights are maroon and burgundy, then the flowers are all cream-coloured and lavender and amethyst. He created some of the flowers on top with chocolate and they're those same light colours, but he also has real violets here, and real pansies here, then you can see the lavender sprigs here." Eva watched her wife's familiar hand trace the colours of the beautiful cake and felt the colours pour into her mind's eye as she went. *We're getting good at this*, she didn't say. The baker had been watching too, and when Eva moved the camera up to catch his kind, round face, his eyes shimmered even in black and grey.

"It's perfect," Eva said to him, and he nodded. When Dev pulled out her wallet, the baker shook his head.

"Not today, *amore mio*. That was too beautiful. Today, it is yours. A gift, as that was to me." He loaded the cake carefully into the Jeep, and hugged them both tightly.

The drive home was soft and warm and quiet. Eva filmed it all.

*E*va lay in bed with her eyes closed while Dev moved around the room getting ready. She opened the closet and surveyed her options, closed the door without choosing anything, her bare feet quiet on the wood floors, until she stepped on *that* spot, and she drew in a short, sharp breath, probably looking over at Eva in their bed to see if she'd been disturbed. Eva didn't move. Dev stood still a little longer, maybe drawing her eyes over the garment rack, maybe looking at Eva lie too still in the bed, clearly awake and pretending not to be. After a moment, Dev returned to the closet and pulled out three hangers, moving them to a hook near their bedroom door. She pulled out a pair of shoes and set them underneath the clothes, then crossed to the bed. Her lips brushed softy against Eva's forehead.

"I set out an outfit for you like you asked, my love," she whispered. "It's those high-waisted, blue-and-green tartan pants you love, with a navy turtleneck and your dark-grey blazer. Your black suede ankle boots are there too." Eva didn't open her eyes yet, didn't respond, but pushed her head against Dev's face slightly. Dev stayed, brought her hand to Eva's jawline, stroked her cheek softly with her thumb. *You've got this*, she didn't say, because Eva was not a pep talk kind of woman. "I love you," she said instead, lingering until she felt the muscles of Eva's jaw relax, felt the weight of her wife's head rest back fully into the pillow. As she passed through the doorway, Eva whispered *thank you* behind her. Dev paused. "Call me if you need anything at all," she said, and heard Eva's head brushing against the pillow in a nod.

From the bed, Eva listened to Dev put on her coat and shoes, leave their house, lock the door behind her. At last she opened her eyes, the dark static under her eyelids replaced by the cloudy, shapeless dark of her bedroom. The March sun had not yet risen, and Dev had made sure to turn all the lights off before she left. When it was dark, Eva had told her, the blindness didn't feel so much like blindness; in the light, the foggy shadowscapes still felt like they were teasing her, a deceptive dynamicity that felt like taking an extra step at the bottom of a flight of stairs, turning her head toward a light but seeing nothing different, foot thudding into unexpected ground.

Once the details had started to leave her, they disappeared quickly: she'd had less than a year left with her sight, filming every moment of it, watching and rewatching the footage in the camera, memorizing every shadow, every shade of grey, every sound and its matching movement until she could just listen, until listening was watching, until it played on the insides of her eyelids on loop. And it had been a year since she'd stopped, a year of learning her house anew, a year of putting off acceptance in favour of an agreed-upon wallow. *Please don't make me learn to live with this yet*, she had not needed to ask. And so her glasses remained on the bedside table, atop the stack of large-print books she had not been able to read for over two years; and so her contacts and contact solution remained in their cluttered medicine cabinet; and so her writing desk remained untouched, notebooks and pencils organized neatly in their proper compartments, useless to her. Dev's patience had astonished her, each conversation had only once—*I won't ask about it again, so just let me know when you want to come back to this*—with a gentleness that filled her chest like the deepest breath she'd ever taken, with certainty: *we have the rest of our lives to get where we're going, and we will.*

Eva swung her legs out of bed and felt for her slippers. She stood slowly, taking her robe from its hook beside the headboard, the silk cool and refreshing. She breathed deeply, exhaled slowly, walked over to the outfit Dev had hung up for her. Her arm extended, she felt for the clothes: the coarse wool of the pants filled her mind with the familiar tartan; the turtleneck was her favourite, soft and clingy in exactly the right way; the blazer was crisp, recently ironed. It was the perfect outfit. She pulled her arm back and closed her eyes, held her hands together at her sternum and relaxed into the static, into an imagined embrace, into the comfort Dev had sewn into the very air of their home. She opened her eyes again and moved through the fog to get ready.

Downstairs, Eva sat in their window nook with a cup of coffee and leaned her head against the glass, imagining the people walking by, with their dogs, with their families, listened for the differences between the trucks and the cars driving past, listened for the car that would pull into their driveway carrying a journalist and her photographer. She had run through her answers to the questions they had emailed her a few days earlier, she had practised all the poses Dev had helped her with, she had imagined the interview to death. *Oh yeah, such an honour to be the youngest nominee for this lifetime achievement award, but also I'm forty-one and blind!* had been her starting point, and the closer it got to eleven o'clock the more she wanted to abandon her whole script. She pulled out her phone and FaceTimed Dev. She picked up instantly.

"Hello love—" and Eva let the audible hitch in Dev's breath pull a grin across her face, pull a giggle from her throat. "Baby, you're a vision," Dev said in a rush. "Your hair is perfect, and your *eyes—*" and Eva heard the way her lips turned up in her sweet, soft smile, heard the way her eyes crinkled at the edges and her eyebrows rose just a little higher into her brow, heard the shimmer in her beautiful brown eyes. She thought she heard a quiet *wow*, a rustle, and then, "Are you alright? Do you need something?" and she heard the risen eyebrows furrow, just a little.

"I'm okay," she said. "Just waiting for them to get here and I wanted to hear your voice. How's your morning been?" And while Dev talked, Eva felt herself relax into the curves and edges of her voice, felt the buzz that had been building all morning subside to a hum. Each time a car slowed in front of their house, she tilted her head toward the driveway and Dev stopped for a moment, until Eva shook her head and Dev continued. Finally, a slowing car turned, and Eva exhaled sharply, nodding. "They're here," she said, and Dev made a kissing sound into the phone.

"I love you," Dev said. "You're amazing."

"I love you, too. Thank you for everything." They hung up and Eva heard the car doors close in the driveway, heard the trunk open. She set her coffee down, then picked up her phone again. She dictated a text to Dev: *Oh, I forgot: could you pick up that Braille textbook on your way home today?*

Grace: bleeding

*I*t was the seventh time this month that she'd seen him: tall and lanky and impeccable, always dressed in a beautiful suit or jacket. This was probably why she noticed him, his square shoulders and crisp clothes standing out among the usual gallery-goers' Blundstones and flannel. She couldn't help but watch him sometimes, the way he dialed his whole body into a conversation, the relaxed attentiveness of his flawless features, the shine of his dark brown eyes that could catch her eye even from across the room. Tonight, she decided, *it cannot go on like this*. She pulled the sleeves of her turtleneck down to cover the bruises in the crooks of her arms, she charted her path.

Her skirt brushed against his jeans as they admired the same sculpture. When he turned to apologize, a flicker of recognition passed over his smooth face. He faltered just long enough for her to mirror the expression, to initiate the apology, to set the course.

"I'm pretty sure I've seen you more than I've seen most of my friends this month," she said with a smile, "and I thought maybe it was time to just introduce myself." He laughed, a round and polished laugh that pulled his mouth into a picture-perfect smile, dimples and all. He stretched a hand out toward her.

"Olu," he said. She took his hand, lightly callused, in a firm grip.

"Grace," she said.

"Are we friends now, then?" he said, eyes sparkling, with their hands still clasped.

"I hope so," she said.

They fell so easily into a routine that within weeks it was hard to imagine a time they hadn't been attending events together: meeting early at a coffee shop, walking to the gallery or the bar or the bookstore, and afterwards finding somewhere to sit, to talk for hours about the event, about what they loved, about what inspired them. He talked about his clients, emerging artists he represented at a small arts agency, and his face shone when he shared the agency's success stories. Grace talked around herself, fit together pieces of her truth to make something more interesting for him, something more resembling a girl, a writer, a love interest. As she layered the truths atop one another she noted the gaps, the seams, kept a mental map for herself, of the Grace she was handing over to Olu.

When the weather warmed, they would walk together after events, aimlessly, arms close and the air sparking between them, but it was weeks before Grace finally led their walk to the house where she rented an attic apartment. She had cleaned it for hours before leaving, scrubbing the blood off the floor, covering the stains on the upholstery with all the blankets she could find, leaving a pile of new books out on the coffee table, leaving the word processor on display on her prized mahogany desk. Her couch was small and her drinks were strong and when Olu asked what kind of writer she was, she finally allowed herself an uncensored truth:

"You know, just a writer like all the other writers— depressed and always a little too ready to bleed out," and he smiled an already-familiar smile, just soft enough to dismiss her morbid humour—never so much of a smile that she could think he agreed, but just enough that they could both let it go without Grace having to apologize. There was so much that was familiar about him, the perfect romantic lead, embodying every heroic kindness and patience and grace, and she had so easily shown him the parts of herself that she knew he could slip into. *Let me make it easy for you*, giving him ambition and passion and a cruel wit that his soft heart could never admit to wanting. *Let me make it easy for you*, closing the distance between them, holding each of his doubts for just long enough that they could dispel them together, keeping them out of sight once they were gone. *Let me make it easy for you*, slipping her hand around his neck and pulling him into her, showing him he was right to want this, showing him she was right.

*I*n the stark halls of the hospital, Olu checked his phone. Angie from the agency had texted him again: *Have you talked to her? She still hasn't gotten back to me. Is everything okay?* It was stupid how fast he and Grace had jumped into their relationship. They'd barely known each other six months, and they were already basically living together. And now he's the go-between, the answer to *What happened to Grace?*

He walked back into the room where Grace lay in bed and sat down beside her. The silence between them was heavy and dark, overpowered by a palpable, enraged resentment. *We are in a hospital*, it said. *This will have to wait until we're home.*

"You shouldn't have brought me here again," Grace said quietly after a nurse left her bedside. "I would have been fine." On her way out of their curtained area, the nurse placed a hand on Olu's shoulders. They exhaled together. He held his response deep in a hollowed chest. The silence grew.

"Did you hear me?"

"I heard you."

"And?"

"I'm going to find a vending machine."

The silence swelled; Olu left.

The nurses nodded at him as they passed, and he smiled back. Sometimes they would ask after him and his clients: the hospital specialized in treating artists, so everyone from the agency was a familiar face here. And now, Grace was too.

Seems like she lost her phone—do you want me to tell her? Angie would have understood the truth, an entirely unremarkable truth, but already he was protective of Grace, already willing to cover up the unremarkable, uncovered truth. (*She worked too long again, we're at the hospital on IV for a bit.*) They are always so ready to die, Angie would say, they'd said a hundred times over their short careers. They are always so unwilling to be kept alive.

Before going back to Grace's bed, he stopped at the nurses' station to collect her things and confirm that they would be able to leave soon, but Grace was already out of bed and shrugging into her jacket when Olu pulled the curtain back. He held up the clear plastic bag with Grace's phone, wallet, and keys; she brushed past him to leave.

In the car on the way to her apartment, the silence burst.

"Was it worth it? Again?"

"I'm not your fucking client, Olu, you don't need to be so goddamn paranoid about it."

"Sure, right, I should care about you, my girlfriend, less than I care about my clients. Makes sense."

"If you love something let it go, right?" Grace's tone was poisonous, but Olu stayed silent; he'd learned Grace's lobs were not worth returning.

Grace immediately cleaned and put away the word processor when she got home, before starting on the tedious task of getting dried blood out of furniture and fabric. She dabbed conscientiously at a bloodstain on the carpet and ignored Olu. Olu watched. The sinewy resentment from the hospital had settled into the currents of Grace's apartment, tightened around each body, held them apart, stationary. But the fight had passed, unfought. Now, she cleaned, dedicated and sterile and cold, and Olu suffocated.

"I know my limits—"

"You don't give a shit about your limits. Passing out isn't a good indicator of when to stop."

Grace's dabbing hardened into a scrubbing.

Olu opened the clear plastic bag from the hospital and threw Grace's phone onto the couch beside where she was scrubbing, dabbing. He stood to leave.

"Angie's been trying to get ahold of you all day." Grace's dabbing—scrubbing—paused: was a vibrating anticipation. Grace reached for her phone and looked at Olu, looked, for the first time, at the anger there in the muscles of his jaw, at the fear there in the shadows of his eyes, looked away from the sadness, there in all the highlights of his beautiful face. "She got an offer for *Poplar City*."

Olu did not wait to look at the ecstasy and devastation that ripped through Grace's body, did not wait for the apology contorting her face, did not offer to celebrate the acceptance of her first manuscript.

Olu left.

*T*he three years since she'd signed the contract for her debut novel had been a whirlwind of good luck; successful events, high-profile endorsements, and a few notable awards lists bolstered Grace's ego to an unrecognizable degree. She had written and sold her second novel in a frenzy, and used the advance toward a down payment on a beautiful apartment downtown with Olu. After several unbearable weeks of hype, early reviews of her new book were finally rolling out, and she had been rooted to the floor of their bedroom, phone in hand, for hours.

Despite herself, Grace scrolled back up to the top of the page and started reading the review again.

"*No Bridge Unburned*, Grace Hart's second book and one of the year's most anticipated titles, I could not have found more predictable if I'd been given a summary beforehand. Despite being a quarter the length of her previous novel, and ten times more densely populated with characters, *No Bridge Unburned* felt passive, empty, and thick. What was once was inventive and unique now, in her second book, comes off as out of touch, stale, and boring, no matter how well she's written it.

"Every character may as well be a clone or close friend of the two characters from *Poplar City,* and Hart's prose between the two books is interchangeable. A part of me almost believes that, if so inclined, one could compare the two novels side by side and find a significant number of repeated lines—verbatim. Regardless, *No Bridge Unburned* is, now, probably the year's biggest flop for me. What could have been an adventurous and elegant look at modern love and suffering instead became a tedious and ostentatious pity party with Grace Hart herself at the centre."

All of the reviews were the same: that she had written a shorter version of her debut, that she had disappointed them, that she had already expired. She declined another call from her agent while she scrolled, brushed aside the text notification from Olu (*Are you okay? Angie called me, she said she hasn't been able to reach you. I'm going to be home as soon as I can*), Googled her name again. She declined a call from the building intercom, and then ignored the knock on the door when whoever it was had gotten into the building anyway. A bruise was forming on her thigh where she was driving her fist into the muscle steadily, rhythmically, mindlessly while she read.

Every time she set her phone down, it was unlocked in her hands again within moments, her thumb mechanically swiping through all the open tabs. She felt a fog coat her eyes and did not look away, she felt the words scrolling by and she heard them from memory even as she didn't register the screen. She didn't need the screen anymore.

Finally she set the phone on the floor beside her and dug the nails of her right hand deep into the soft, bruised skin in the bend of her left elbow. The pain shone through her whole body, tingling, spiderwebbing into the base of her skull, and then it throbbed, working its way back toward the source. She pressed harder, leaned into the relief of it, felt tears form in her eyes, pressed harder until she cried out and let her arms fall limply. It had dulled. It had all dulled, and in the dullness she located her legs, her feet, she pushed herself to standing and met her half-closed eyes in the mirror, she pulled her slack face into a calm and lifeless gaze, she set her shoulders. She called Angie, she called Olu, she was okay, she had been sleeping, she was okay, she would talk to them later. She walked out to her mahogany desk in the living room and threw the word processor to the floor, where it clattered and left a dent in the hardwood. She opened her laptop and began searching Facebook.

In university, she had tried to supplement her grocery store wages with a poorly managed freelance editing gig, helping other students with their papers, until she had been interrupted on her way to class one morning by a burly kid in a Wu-Tang hat who warned her not to steal his clientele. Unbeknownst to her, word had been spreading that she would *write* papers, and her going rate was a fraction of his. Of course, she had stopped immediately, haunted for weeks by the fear that she would be caught and punished for almost participating in plagiarism. Since she had not, in fact, been trying to encroach on Wu-Tang boy's demographic, they had become a strange kind of friends, Grace's quivering perfectionism humming alongside his easy brilliance. Through him, she learned about so many of the ways people broke the rules, and she was amazed by how easy he made it seem.

She found him on Facebook and he responded quickly with his number, which she called just as quickly. The scope of his services had expanded since university, as had his network, and he confirmed the rumours: black-market blood worked. Writers strapped for cash could sell bags of their blood, and using it would overpower your own creativity with theirs. He assured her that his dealer vetted the writers for talent, and she almost asked if they were vetted for disease, too, but decided she didn't care. He gave her a time, a place, a phone number, and the price.

Grace stared at the case of blood on her desk. She wondered briefly if it was as easy to buy cocaine as it was to buy blood. She rubbed the rough skin in the crook of her elbow; she wondered if it was easier.

The case was heavy, sloshing, closed. Grace's own blood was everywhere in the apartment: dried into her chair, staining the floor around her desk, embedded in her clothes, Olu's clothes, their linens. Grace's blood was a ubiquitous furnishing in their lives. But occasionally, Olu would come home with someone else's blood on his suit—from a reproduction factory, from a photo shoot, from a careless client—and it would repulse her. The brownness of it, the stink, the flippant disregard for professionalism. A jealousy she couldn't admit to would weigh on the back of her mind until, inevitably,

"Can't you just be more fucking careful? Jesus, Olu. Look at your fucking sleeves."

Grace closed her eyes as she opened the case. She blindly placed a hand atop the contents, which squished thickly, cool to the touch. She gagged. She turned her head and opened her eyes: 6:07. If she took the sauce out of the freezer right now, it might thaw in the saucepan by 8:30. She flexed her fingers and felt the blood bags shift.

(Olu would be home at eight. He would be tired from a day of factory tours with his artists; he would hope Grace would have the evening planned out, begun.)

Olu had spent the weekend cleaning—the word processor shone on Grace's writing desk, keys uncaked, even the type-tube clear as new. She sat down with the modification, opened up the instructions from an incognito window on her phone. It clicked in easily—she wondered how many illegal parts fit so invisibly into their previous constraints. She connected the IV tube to the modification.

(He had sent Grace a text that morning reminding her to take the spaghetti sauce out of the freezer. He would want meatballs from the Italian deli, would want a Caesar salad and red wine. He would not want dessert, the pasta and croutons being enough of a cheat. He would hope it would all be started by the time he got home.)

6:14. The deli was just around the corner, but she always forgot to account for the time getting her shoes on, finding her keys, waiting for the elevator. Always five, ten minutes late. If she left now, she would get home in time to clean up the day's small messes before starting dinner. She could buy more sauce with the meatballs. She could even get garlic bread. If she left now.

(Olu had texted at three to remind her of their ten o'clock session with the nutritionist and personal trainer. He would want the place to be tidy in order to make a good first impression. He would want Grace to be at least equally enthusiastic about following through with their new, mutually approved commitment. He would want Grace to smile, to shake hands, to sit up straight. To talk.)

She sat down at her desk and hooked up her word processor, slipped the iv into the crook of her elbow and hooked the other end into the power slot. Opened the valve from the stolen blood. Waited; frowned; flinched; convulsed.

The new writer wasn't quiet about entering her bloodstream: she seethed; she boiled. She turned her rage from the inside out and back in again: she hated her bookshelf, she hated her haircut, she hated Olu's pristine half of the closet. She closed her eyes and tried to relax her accidental fists, slowed her lungs into the tiniest bellows, afraid and in awe of the fire. She was relieved to find out there was so much more to hate than herself. She let her open palms rest on the keys in front of her.

(If dinner wasn't ready, Olu wouldn't be mad. He would ask what had kept her busy this afternoon; was she working on something new? Olu was never mad, always trying to find a window of opportunity for sympathy or understanding. He would heat up soup or make eggs for both of them. He wouldn't even slam the cutlery and dishes around. He would forget to take his tie off; he would quietly hand Grace her dinner and ask her to choose the entertainment for dinner.)

Olu's voice in the hallway ripped her eyes open—8:07. The case sat open on the bed, and a small puddle of blood had formed on her desk where the hookup had started to leak. Eight hundred words bled in and out of focus as she fumbled with the IV, trying not to make more of a mess pulling it out. The woman in 1706 was telling Olu about her grandson's recent student photography prize. Blood streamed out of her elbow, onto the carpet, the duvet, trembling hands slamming shut the case, shoving it under her side of the bed.

(Olu's key turned in the lock.)

Hart's third novel is exactly nothing like the book I expected to sit down with and review this spring. Gone are the pages of meandering introspection, the unmotivated cast, the predictably hopeless dead-end jobs. The flourishes, the floundering—the semicolons!—the very essence of a Hart novel is completely absent from And Another, *and let me tell you: she couldn't have made a better decision.* And Another *marks a visionary turn in what was threatening to become another stale career.*

"This is not Grace Hart," I first exclaimed when I read through the first several chapters of the novel. I was so thrown that I nearly put the book down right then and there, but something motivated me—persuaded me to keep reading. First it was intellectual curiosity—how does a writer so completely change her style, so beautifully, so flawlessly? From intellectual curiosity it was a short leap to sheer appreciation for Hart's

complete mastery of the English language—in a completely different way than she flaunted in her debut, and which floundered in her sophomore novel. With And Another, *Hart subverts every expectation in a tour de force, and in doing so, just like she has done before, redefines literary writing.*

*S*he knew she was brooding. She knew it wasn't worth brooding over—some kid on a blog who'd completely missed the point. Her fourth book had already made all of the great critical splashes it needed to make. After the crushing success of *And Another*, after a tour spent fearing that the writer whose blood really wrote the book would stand up during the Q&A and unravel Grace's uncharacteristically clumsy web of deceit, she had made a deal with herself: succeed or fail on her own terms. And now her fourth book had already succeeded—and it had failed this kid, this blog.

She knew it wasn't worth reading again, worth memorizing, worth complaining about. But she was on her third drink and it was only barely noon and Olu had said he'd be back in time for lunch and what was there to do *other* than read it again, pour another glass, wait for a target to walk through the door.

I'm sorry Grace. You know how it is, just try to put it out of your head.

Sometimes she wondered what it felt like to be Olu's client, if it felt the same. Sometimes, when she got these manicured one-liners after a confessional text (*I know I'm being stupid but that kid's review is really getting to me*), when their emotional transactions were so careful, it made her wonder. Was she just another professional liability, just another moody writer leaning a little too hard on an agent? Olu, always so careful. How comforting an agent he would be.

Okay, well how about this: I'll move things around and come home at lunch. Let's go to a movie.

Sometimes she wondered if she was a coward. (*I'd really like that, thank you.*) Sometimes she didn't have to wonder: scrolling through her message conversations, opening one with an unsaved number, *Hey. Thinking of you today. Thursday can't come soon enough.*

By the time Olu arrived home shortly after noon she was Friday-night drunk and she didn't want to see him anymore. Olu's kisses are long and soft and tender every time and every time his hands were gentle and loving and every time she could feel Olu's kindness spilling into her body in that kiss and on days like this day the kindness made her want to die: slurring in the passenger seat on the way to an early Tuesday movie; watching Olu decline a call from a client; not choosing the movie; not saying *I'm sorry, thank you.*

After the movie, Olu checked his phone: four missed calls and a voicemail, all from one client. In the car on the way home, the voicemail echoed into the space between them: "Hey Olu. Sorry to bother you—I hope you're having a really good day. I was just calling to ask you a bit more about the gallery. You know, I'm trying to work on that new series of canvases, but it's just not really clicking. I think...well, I don't want to disappoint you, Olu. Or anyone. So I'm just...Anyway I hope it doesn't cause too much trouble. Sorry again. Hope you're having a nice afternoon. I really appreciate the faith you've had in me. Say hi to Grace."

Outside the house, Olu stayed in the car. "I want to go check in on my client," he said, nodding at his phone. Even then his kiss was long and soft and tender. "Will you be okay?" he asked. Grace knew she should do more than shrug. But she shrugged, stepped out of the car, walked into their home. Olu left.

The funeral was on a Thursday. Olu had not asked her for anything, had not asked her to stop crying about it, had not asked her to give him the space to grieve. "You don't have to come," Olu had said to her as soon as he had helped the family finalize the date. "I'll be busy most of the time anyway, and I know it might make you feel awkward to be alone." Somehow, he was still so soft, comforting and quiet every night: his palm gentle against Grace's cheek, his lips against the crown of her head, the kindest *Are you okay?* in the warmest embrace. As though it shouldn't have been her doing the holding, the asking. As though it shouldn't have been her doing something, anything at all.

Every day Olu had offered Grace a way out and every day she had done the right thing and refused it.

(How long are you willing to watch a person fail to act?)

But Thursday morning arrived: "I'm so sorry, Olu. I don't think I can come with you today—" headache, nausea, exhaustion, anxiety, depression. Neither of them needed a specific excuse. "Don't forget the cleaners are coming at ten, since I just haven't been able to keep up this past week." Olu (still soft, still tender) left, and he locked the door behind him, and Grace pulled out her phone and texted a go-ahead to the unsaved number in her messages.

And the cleaners came at ten, left at eleven, and at noon Grace opened the door for a beautiful man in jeans and a plaid shirt and offered him a drink. He groped her thoughtlessly as he walked by, let himself onto the balcony, lit a cigarette.

The man behind the unsaved number was everything Olu had never been and which Grace loved Olu for never becoming: his lips were hard and impatient, his uncallused hands rough and unforgiving. His wiry body had no patience for her minute adorations, for her contortive insecurities. With this man, Grace's role was clear to her, a role so easy to slip into, a role Olu spent every day of their lives encouraging her to grow out of. As the man sat across from her on the balcony and smoked, self-loathing and subservience replaced the aching anxiety of living up to Olu's expectations, and Grace relaxed into this new—old, same, different—shame working its way through her veins.

(Not a dramatic failing: a simple not doing, a doing something else, an avoidance.)

The man left and Grace stepped into a shower that seared her skin lobster-red and she sat in the bathtub and watched her body turn the colour of a new sunburn in the falling water and she folded her arms and moved her fingers over the callused skin in the crooks of her elbows and felt nothing but a full-body sting. She experimented with how long she could stand the drumming of the water before shifting, hiding, moving the target.

The air in the bathroom was sticky and hot but still cold against her pink skin. She was grateful for the fog on the mirror as she pulled on clean clothes, and avoided her own blurry eyes anyway. She stepped out of the bathroom and stopped, stared at Olu on the balcony sitting where the other man had sat, holding the glass the other man had drunk from, hunched over the ashtray. She stared at Olu not at a funeral. Even like this he was the most beautiful man, even with these unfamiliar slouched shoulders, even with his back turned, even with a tremor rippling through his body as he sat. She stared and drank in Olu's unquenchable beauty and felt it finally rip her to pieces and felt her loathing rush to fill the cracks in what she had finally broken. She walked to the balcony.

(How long before you overtake them?)

"You're home early."

He didn't even start, just straightened his shoulders and shifted to look at her. Grace hated absolutely noth-ing about Olu except the way he asked her to be her best self, every day, his relentless hope that they could con-tinue to grow together, except the way he forgave her every time she failed him. She had failed him too often. She would not grow. Her best self was a shadow of his. The gap between them, the gap he refused to acknowledge, was insurmountable. She would never be good enough— she would prove it.

(How many times will you teach a person to fish, to stand, to wash dishes, to make spaghetti?)

"Did you have someone over?" Olu asked, and his voice was tight and they both knew what an affair looked like and still Olu asked her: *Be your best self. Be honest.*

Grace watched herself make the wrong choice. "Just someone from my writing group, he was having a hard day." As though Olu wasn't having a hard day, as though she hadn't made a meaningless excuse to avoid accompanying him to a funeral, as though she had done a kind thing. And Olu's disappointment rippled through his whole body, and she waited, she waited for him to tell her that she'd been selfish, but of course he just nodded his head and set down the other man's glass and stood and told her, "I have to go back for the reception. Just wanted to check in. Do you want to join me? I can wait for you to get dressed if you want."

She could say yes, she could put on one of her myriad black outfits and she could wrap her arm around Olu's waist and she could press her forehead into his shoulder, tell him *You are such a good man*. She could say *I'm sorry, I'm still not feeling well*, she could hold his beautiful face in her hands and kiss him softly and tell him he was such a good man, tell him she would have dinner ready for them both in the evening. She could say anything.

"You don't need to check in on me. I'm fine. Just go."

(How many times will a person say *I'm sorry*?)

Grace's chest heaved with the effort of stopping the fight, the fight she'd started, the one-sided interminable fight of making Olu hate her, too. She stared at him and they stared at the wreckage and refused to name it: the tumbler and ashtray in pieces on the carpet, the wall dusted with ash. Grace's violence and Olu's sighs and the other man's cologne still filled the air, for once an odour stronger than the ubiquitous blood. Soft and pleasant, a stinging undertone and finish. Olu grabbed a broom.

Grace yelled, and yelled, and yelled.

Olu poured the broken glass into the garbage bin.

Olu left.

Grace yelled, and yelled.

The End

In which a story begins

Finn: a mother

*F*inn clicked "send" angrily before rereading the email to her ex-husband: *Have you seen this? This is what happens when you try to stop your kid from doing something they love. I'm taking them to the safety workshop next week, and really don't care what you think.* She clicked the link again, and let the video play one more time. Her kid sat across from a girl in their grade twelve class, in an oddly framed interview setup. The girl welcomed viewers by saying how excited they were to have the one and only Paige Callaghan on their show, drummer and vocalist for none other than that year's battle-of-the-bands winner. (Finn hadn't known there was a band, or a battle, hadn't known that Paige had won.) She chewed her fingers and agonized one more time over her Paige's unbelievable, terrifying, and devastatingly genuine interview answers.

"I mean yeah, it hurts. Like, you can see my arms: it even looks like it hurts. Ha, yeah, it's pretty gross, but, you know: I literally tear one of the bones out so I can smash it against a drum kit. There are two bones in each forearm, right, so I use one and leave one in.

"No, it's okay to look. I mean, nobody really does." Paige held their arms out to the person at the camera, daring, goading them to zoom in. "It's so gross, right, so I think people think it's rude? And other drummers don't really need to look, like we know already. And even, other artists or musicians—I think everyone has something, if not arms like this then it's just something else nobody is really looking at. So it sort of feels like carrying around an elephant in the room, but in every room, all the time. And I'm at this point where, if I have to carry around this elephant, I'm going to just let it do what it wants. Because who cares?" The interviewer was rapt, something like a horrified admiration spilling out of her dark-rimmed eyes. Finn shuddered at Paige's sheer force of being alive.

"So I guess that's how I do it. I just do. I want to make music, and this is the only way I can—to break shit. I'm good at breaking shit: my bones, other people's noses, my grandpa's china, my mother's spirit." Finn snorted despite herself. "I think that people assume it's because I'm reckless, or careless, or even just young. Or that they think being reckless and careless—and young—are the same thing. But it takes a lot of work to punch a hole in the wall, you know? You've got to get past two pretty serious logical objections: first, this is going to hurt my hand, possibly needing immediate medical attention; second, I will need to either fix or explain the hole in the wall. And then you need to really commit to this completely illogical reaction. Lots of people will punch a wall, semi-committed, and walk away with both their hand and the wall intact. But me, I'll commit to it. I see your serious logical objections and raise you a broken fucking hand, because I don't want to go unacknowledged. I'll start the fight. I'll slice open my arm and rip the bone out, because I'm not just going to sit around and wait for someone else to say—or make, or do—what I want to say." Finn mouthed the words along with the video and hit replay then pause as soon as it ended. She breathed haltingly and loudly through her nose, checked for a response from her ex. The dog had tiptoed over to the desk and nudged his wet nose into the back of her knee. She set a hand on the soft fur right behind his ears and sighed. She clicked play.

*T*he café was large but crowded: with easels, with writing desks, with instruments, with art, with cleaning supplies, with bookshelves and board games and tables and chairs. A large poster, for first-timers, hung beside the menu boards.

WELCOME TO ARTS N CATS

Where everyone is welcome

except people who don't respect the rules

1. Respect the cats. They live here; you don't. If they don't want your lovin', don't force it. Friendly reminder that this also applies to humans.

2. Respect the staff. They spend a lot more time here than you. We don't abide by the stupid rule of retail where the customer is always right.

3. Respect each other. There's a lot going on here at any given time: respect the shared space, stay quiet in the quiet areas, clean up your mess, and don't be a jerk.

A chalkboard near the back of the room showed the week's scheduled events, from punk shows to open mics to typography classes to their free weekly safety workshops, different specialties guest-hosted by local artists each week and mandatory for regulars. A smaller poster advertised the weekly meetings for parents with artistic kids, to teach them about safety and support—but all the patrons figured it was just a place parents got together to complain about their careless, reckless, irresponsible teenagers.

Finn loved her hosting week at Arts N Cats. Every few months she would get in touch with the owner to get herself on the schedule. Sometimes the kids knew who she was, sometimes they didn't. There was a particular joy in getting a group of fresh-faced visual artists or writers, with no idea who she was other than a barrier between them and a free workspace. It was nice to be nobody.

But today, she was Mom, and Paige was grudgingly drinking in the irresistible charm of Arts N Cats. Someone had forgotten to close the French doors that separated the visual arts studio from the rest of the space, and Beethoven—a new light-footed kitten with no boundaries and an abundance of curiosity—had snuck in to watch the few teenagers at work. The manager came out from the back room and waved at Finn. Beethoven's ears pricked at the sound of the back door closing, and he scuttled out of the workroom. On his way out, he dashed through a puddle of blood under one kid's easel, tracking tiny murderous paw prints through the main seating area and into the feline-only forest, a modest arrangement of small trees, scratching posts, and cat beds. Finn saw Paige smile quickly, and was careful not to be caught staring.

The back room of the café filled slowly with teenagers who agonized over where to sit. The room came alive with hushed chatter and hesitant introductions. A young woman stood at the front of the room and rubbed her arms nervously, over rough red skin and barely healed gashes. Finn involuntarily brought her own hand to the scar on her chest, smooth and faded. She felt again that it was no wonder Paige never talked to her about their music—she had nothing to show for herself anymore but licensing cheques and a soft white line between her ribs.

At four o'clock, the owner popped his head into the room and bellowed: "Alright drummers, you know the drill: pay attention, pass the quiz, and sign out with me when you're done so you can use the studio spaces next time you come in. Don't forget the rules. Take it away, Mick."

Paige talked excitedly their entire drive home.

"Did you see her at all? God, she was so cool. I can't believe I actually got to meet Mick Archer. You should have told me that's who was leading this thing! Don't you remember when she came here on tour a few years ago? She's such a badass. She just doesn't give a shit what anyone thinks, you know?" It had been so long since Paige had said this much to her at once. She tried to bask without seeming to bask, to respond just enough to keep the monologue going. "And—oh, man, she talked about her thing, that thing she opens her shows with, do you remember?"

She had to stop herself from cringing at the memory. One of the first times she'd really crossed the bridge to being an embarrassing mom. Paige had been fourteen, and their group of friends was going to this punk show. She knew fourteen was old enough, but she'd bought herself a ticket anyway and hung back from the group and she'd been awed and terrified by their chaos, their unbridled energy, their rage, she'd been so proud to know kids were still angry, her kid was so angry. And that opening act, that signature move—it was the closest she'd come to ripping her own heart out again after that show.

In the elevator up to the apartment, Paige shuffled, touching their forearms lightly and trying to covertly glance over at Finn.

"Mom?"

"Yeah?"

"Why did you stop?"

Finn breathed in sharply. Nobody had asked her that in over a decade; she'd forgotten her answer. Her hand rested against her own faded scar under her sweater, Paige's gaze boring into her as they walked down the hall. In the apartment, she sat on the couch. She still hadn't answered.

"Honestly?"

"Duh."

"It was so hard—"

Paige's face crumpled, and Finn hated herself for her fractional truth.

"No, wait. It was too much. It turned into something that wasn't me, or mine, and it still hurt so badly but I wasn't even being truthful anymore. I never really meant to stop…Well, I still think of doing it again sometimes. Why do you ask?" Paige perched on an armrest across from her, quiet.

"In the workshop before the safety stuff, Mick Archer talked a bit about, you know, our inspirations or whatever. She had this slideshow with her favourite musicians and writers and stuff. You were in it—this picture of you and Grandma, at a gallery maybe?" Paige was quiet again for a moment, staring at their hands and picking at their old nail polish. "You looked so different."

In her office, Finn slouched over the photo albums spread out on her desk. She knew the picture, the moment. Remembered the bickering on the drive to the ceremony, but now too remembered how Cleo was so good to her that night. Always so good at protecting her, always the problem. In the photo, her mother's body was closer to the camera than hers, their hands clasped tightly, Cleo's gaze steeled directly into the lens. Such a desperate relief to have it directed outward for once. Cleo's face bore the weight of their whole family in her crows' feet, in her mouth that turned downwards but still conveyed a gentle smile, in the cautious, hopeful arches in her eyebrows, in that icy blue fire. They had been laughing and she remembered her mother's laugh—picturesque, laden with a sadness you didn't want to look at too closely—and she remembered her mother's sadness, her mother's impossibly small hands, defiantly strong hugs, her tender and perfect grasp.

At Mick Archer's show, Finn had cradled her scar and remembered her mother. She had watched while the band took their places. In a foggy darkness Mick had climbed up to the platform with her drums and unwound the gauze from her arms.

When the stage lit up, there she was, standing tall behind her drums with one bone already in her hand and the other in her arm. The singer screamed into the microphone; the bass and guitar slammed into action. And Mick had grabbed the scalpel sitting on the snare drum and sliced through that morning's loose stitches, thrust her bleeding arm above her head.

Rivulets of blood had coated her arm from wrist to shoulder as she shook and stamped to the as-yet non-existent beat of the song, until finally she had raised her empty hand and reached into her forearm. She screamed with the singer when she ripped the bone out, her full body coming down hard on the drums, crashing out the heart of the song. Finn had clawed at her scar; she had felt her lungs burning in her chest, had remembered ripping a body apart for something bigger. She remembered the cruelty of it.

At her desk, Finn started when Paige knocked on the door. "Come in," she called, and added "you scared the shit out of me," when Paige stepped through the doorway. They both smiled crookedly, and Finn was reminded more than ever that this kid was *her* kid. She held out her arm and invited Paige to perch on her knee, a pose they hadn't shared in years. To her surprise, Paige shimmied closer and actually did lower themselves onto Finn's lap. They reached out and spread the photos for a better view.

"Do you miss her?" Paige asked.

"Every day, lately," Finn replied without thinking. She looked at Paige, looking at the photographs. "She would have raked me over the coals for the way I've...*handled* your drumming." They both looked at Cleo, young and fierce and vibrant, on the desk. "Do you remember her?" Paige shook their head.

"You don't talk about her much," they said after a while. "You don't talk about anything from before." Finn filled her weak lungs slowly, held her breath, exhaled even more slowly. She leaned her head against Paige's shoulder, and felt tears well behind her eyes when Paige leaned their head toward her in return.

"I think I messed this up a bit, kid." Paige snorted. "You are this whole incredible human and I think some part of me was scared of that." Finn looked at Cleo, looked at Paige, looked at her younger self on the desk, her scar raw and leaky. *You were the only thing I'd ever loved enough to be scared of losing*, she didn't say. Paige shifted, stood, looked down at Finn with their head cocked. Loss was only barely in their periphery, still. Fear was still something to be conquered.

"I'm going to do better, okay?" Paige didn't nod, but sucked their cheeks in, gnawing the insides.

"Can I come to your next show?" Finn asked, and Paige grimaced, shook their head.

"Absolutely not," they said, and Finn couldn't help but laugh. "But for what it's worth, I think you're already doing great." Paige had turned away almost immediately, rushed out the words on their way out of the office, and Finn's heart had caught in her throat, so by the time she tried to say *I love you*, Paige had already closed the door behind them.

Finn clutched at her chest. *I love you.*

Eva: a partner

*L*ying on her back, Eva could feel the sharp uneven ground of their campsite pressing through the rough wool of the blanket. The leaves and needles of the nearby trees danced loudly in a warm evening breeze—a breeze that carried the familiar scent of saltwater and seaweed, of a bonfire down the beach. Eva let the air pour over her, wind its fingers through the loose hairs around her temples that had escaped her ponytail, stick itself to her bare arms and legs, push its way through her light T-shirt. When the air stilled, Dev and coffee filled her senses: the espresso pot bubbling on the campfire, the dark, sweet roast of the coffee soft and cool in the humid summer evening, Dev's familiar scent underpinning everything. When Eva let her focus lift, their neighbouring campers drifted in—a low, booming laugh, a child's pitter-patter gait, tires on gravel, a hint of a joint, and fires crackling in every direction.

Dev's chair creaked and the bubbling of the espresso quieted. Eva imagined the rich brown, the steam rising from their cups as the coffee poured slowly. Dev's sandals had a particular sound to them, her steps airy and hushed. The blanket rustled as Dev stepped onto it, lowered herself to the ground beside Eva, set the coffee down on the ground above Eva's head. "Behind you," she said quietly, and Eva nodded. She pushed herself up slowly, nestled herself into her wife, found the cup behind her. Dev kissed her forehead, lingered.

"Are you ready?" Dev asked.

"I think so," she said. "It feels ready, the syllabus, the schedule. It all feels ready." She felt Dev smile. *But are you ready?* She didn't ask, and Eva didn't answer. They had spent the year since Eva's public retirement globe-trotting, taking all the vacations they had been putting off and putting off and putting off. Dev took a leave of absence from her work, and it had been a strangely blissful year, filled—for Eva—with the scents and sounds of being alive, of being alive in the Alps, of being alive in Mykonos, of being alive in the Rockies, of being alive in Nashville, of stadium concerts and amphitheatre Shakespeare. It was finding out what snow smells like, how different New Orleans rain feels from Vancouver rain, how the wind in Ireland is hardly even related to the wind in Alaska, but is sibling to the winds of the East Coast Trail. In Montana, on a crisp and bright morning filled with the sounds of a restless lake, she'd received an email letting her know she'd gotten the job she'd applied for at York University, and the abstract unabstracted itself into a September start, into a new career, the beginning of an *after* she'd been skirting around since she first started losing colour. After was here. Or, after started on Tuesday. For now—

"Can we go for a walk?" she asked.

"Of course."

"Will you—"

"Of course."

Eva slid her feet into flip-flops and listened to Dev fold the blanket, put out the fire, tuck their things away in the trunk of the Jeep. Her soft, airy footsteps approached, and the warmth of her was familiar, comforting. Eva slid her arm into her wife's elbow, their sweaty skin tacky, and they laughed at the general unglamour of summer.

"When do you want me to start?" Dev asked as they walked slowly toward the beach.

"Start with the sky," she said.

"It's perfect," Dev started. "The sun is just about gone, but it's still brilliantly orange at the horizon. It's clear today, and the moon is already shining bright and silver over the water. It's almost a perfect half, the kind of moon you like to say is underrated. From the horizon, the sky fades perfectly through yellow, and light blue, and a rich, dark navy is blanketing most of us now. It almost looks the way a sunset looks from a plane, above the clouds. Some of the trees are still drowning in the sunset, and they're so golden it looks like fall."

The gravel path they'd been walking on turned to dirt, then sand, and Eva stopped them to pull off her flip-flops. The sand was still hot from the day, soft and grainy in her toes. The rhythm of the small waves against the shore massaged the muscles of her heart, drew the knots from her jaw, her neck, her shoulders.

"Are there any stars yet?" She felt Dev's head tilt upwards, look around them.

"Not really, not yet, but it's going to be a rave tonight, you can already tell—there are a few out, small and a little dim, but it's still light."

"Tell me about the people."

"There aren't many, but the people who are out here all look like they're having so much fun. There's an older couple at a picnic table that they dressed up fantastically: they brought a blue gingham tablecloth and a classic picnic basket, and it looks like they're having wine right now with...crackers, maybe? Her hair reminds me of my mom's, a perfect French twist at the *beach*, and his hair is perfectly snow white, in a superhero coif. Like if Superman aged, I feel like he might look like this man."

"I'm happy to know that Superman and Lois live a long and happy life together." The distant murmur of a jet ski was followed by a small crash of water against the shore.

"There's also a pair of people walking just ahead of us, with an enormous golden retriever who keeps running into the water and back to them; they're not calling the dog, but they give it a treat every time it comes back. One of them is wearing a fantastic bikini with sunflowers on it, and the other one has a complicated and stunning black one-piece, with lots of straps and cut-outs. God I feel old, Eva."

"Lois and Superman," Eva said.

"Lois and Wonder Woman?" Dev planted a kiss—soft, always soft, she was always so soft—on Eva's cheek and Eva laughed. "You're Wonder Woman, of course," Dev murmured into the top of Eva's head.

"I am without a doubt Lois, my love. I doubt Wonder Woman would have to ask for help rearranging the furniture in her library. And anyway, we're not old. Blind, maybe, achy sometimes, but not old. Tell me about the water."

Back in their tent, they pushed their sleeping bags aside and curled into each other. It was a curling they didn't need to think about, not with almost twenty years of practice, and Eva loved the way it buried her in Dev's presence. This, she didn't need to see; this, she had always only felt, the warmth and the weight of her wife holding her in the dark, of holding her wife. It was too hot to stay like this for long, but they would stay as long as they could.

"Can I test something out on you?" Eva murmured into Dev's collarbone.

"Always." They shuffled, unwound, and Eva lay on her back, eyes closed. She felt Dev prop herself up on one elbow and look down at her.

"I want to say something…inspiring. I think it's probably too much, but I want to set the tone for the course. I want them to know what matters to me." Dev was quiet, but Dev was always quiet when Eva spoke. Dev listened, and Eva knew her attention was dialled into her entirely, could feel it, knew without a doubt that Dev was always listening. *I don't know if I'm ready*, she didn't say. And Dev didn't say *You are*, but they were both right. Eva reached up the arm closest to her wife, searching for fingers to twine together, and when they knotted their hands Eva could feel it, all of it, their whole story and the decades they had yet to go.

She began.

She could feel Dev clinging to each word, each pause, each breath, and she continued, and she let the feeling of Dev's attention sink under her skin. When she finished talking, she listened to Dev's soft breath, to the rustle of Dev lifting her arm to rest a gentle hand against Eva's cheek.

"Will you come with me?" Eva asked quietly.

"I will go to the ends of the earth with you, my love, for as long as you want me."

Grace: a friend

*—Miss Hart, does it ever bother you that you're a cliché?*

—I'm a famous writer, Jada. Is there any way to live that wouldn't be?

—Not alone in the woods would probably be a good start.

—Then I'd just be a different kind of cliché.

She wondered if today would be the day. She held her eyes closed against the intruding sun, watched the day unfold: coffee, porch, walk, get the mail, get the neighbour's mail, stop by the neighbour's, more coffee. It's Wednesday: drive to town, check email at the café, lunch at the diner, visit Eunice. It's the fourteenth: stop by the bookshop, buy books, drop off a cheque. Home, read, coffee, walk, check on Jim and the dogs. Stay for dinner, maybe. Turn down a drink, settle for a cigarette. Home—

It was the first day she could feel the air pricking through her jacket, the first day that could be a scarf day, the reds and yellows clinging desperately, falling wildly, flying for a moment (ecstatic, alone). The skin of her hands bright red, the steam from her coffee pooling between the liquid and the rim of the cup, not standing a chance against the wind. Her fingers burned between the mug and the air. She breathed deeply; the breath hurt.

The neighbour's mailbox was empty, but she stopped in anyway and accepted the coffee and conversation. The coffee was tar, and she drank it and she nodded and she listened: the neighbour's granddaughter was coming up for the weekend and this was nice, it would be nice to see her, but he knew it meant his daughter was off with *him* again and Lord knows what they did—no, he knew, he knew exactly what they did, because the needles would still be on the fucking coffee table when he brought back their little girl, and he wondered if that little girl liked it enough up here to consider moving, he wondered if he could just bring the girls up here and help them settle, but no, his daughter would never go for it. Not without Ethel around anymore.

They both looked toward the rocking chair in the corner of the room, Ethel's chair, her crocheted blanket hanging neatly over its back. It was almost a year ago that Grace had stopped by with the mail and found an ambulance in the driveway, carting away a stretcher covered head-to-toe in a blanket. Peacefully, in her sleep. The neighbour sitting on the stairs, holding a large pink curler in his weathered bare hands.

Grace sighed, stood slowly, took their mugs into the kitchen. She touched the man's bony shoulder lightly, pulling him from a short reverie. "Should be good to see them, though," he said. "You know how it is." Grace nodded.

"I'm heading into town today. You need anything?"

"That's okay, thanks."

She passed over the hearth on her way out and surveyed the room. The rifle had been leaning in the corner behind the recliner for almost a year.

"Thanks for the coffee. I'll see you tomorrow."

—*What are we doing here again?*

—*My writing assignment is to interview another writer. Everyone will be so jealous that I got to interview the* legendary *Grace Hart.*

—*I thought you didn't know any of my books.*

—*I Googled you. My teacher's a big fan.*

An unforgiving wind buffeted her car as she drove along the highway, watching turning leaves tear from their branches, evergreens pushing into each other like dominoes. Clouds rushed through the sky, late for tomorrow, the kind of sky that brings a thunderstorm out of the clear blue. The town sprang up from behind a bend in the road, an infamous bend, slick and blind and unmarked, and then, behind a handful of two-by-four crosses, it appeared.

Death was everywhere here.

The diner and internet café shared a building under a sign that read *Colson's General*, across from the liquor store and sandwiched between a laundromat and the bus station. At 10:15, a small group of parents finished up breakfast after school drop-off; the sheriff stopped by for a donut and to flirt with Margaret behind the counter, who looked like she'd rather be going over the week's sales. Margaret's daughter Jada was unstocking the morning's shipment during her morning spare. The sheriff left, and Margaret furrowed her thin face while she reopened her ledger. Ranchers picked up their feed.

—Tell me about Olu.

—I thought you said you Googled me.

—Google doesn't know anything about love.

—Neither do I.

"Morning, honey," said Margaret as Grace entered the store.

"Morning."

"Cold one today, isn't it."

"I know it means a long winter, but I have to say it's a welcome change."

"I hear you, it's been a hell of a summer."

Grace settled into one of the computers along a window bench amid shelves of tack, tools, feed, and seeds. As she opened her email, Jada wandered over with a mug of coffee.

"Morning, Miss Hart," she said. Her dark hair was pulled back into a tight ponytail that exploded into thick coils.

"Morning, Jada. You know you can call me Grace." Jada smiled, poured Grace's coffee, and perched on a stool beside her. Grace looked up—sometimes, Jada felt like the glue of the whole town, with her strange, sharp mind and her steady commitment to being entirely no-nonsense. You could not help but feel a tenderness, an awe, when Jada was around: she asked for the best of you without asking. She reminded Grace so much of Olu that it hurt sometimes.

"I know, Miss Hart," she said suddenly, and stood just as suddenly, taking the coffee pot to the one other person sitting in the diner. Grace smiled wistfully to herself.

"Thanks for the coffee."

—*Tell me about Olu?*

—*Why is it so important to you? I don't see what this has to do with writing.*

—Of course you do.

—A person can only take so many apologies, I think.

—What was he apologizing for?

—Not him, Jada. He never had to apologize for anything.

She logged off the computer just as a few truckers arrived for an early lunch. She left a pair of twenties underneath her empty mug and pie plate and nodded to Jada and Margaret on the way out. Outside, the clouds had slowed, settled into a wet grey blanket ready to wring itself out over the little downtown. She dropped more coins into her meter and the meters beside her, grabbed a hat from the truck, and headed east past a string of newly smashed storefronts, the latest of the annual fall break-ins—usually kids stocking up and taking a final stab at running away before it got too cold, before running just meant leaving one hell for a different, frozen one. Grace jotted the businesses down in her agenda.

She reached the hotel just as the sky blackened and split open, water rushing to meet the street. It was the hotel that kept them all going, just notable enough to make this particular highway town the highway town to rest at between actual attractions. The security guard buzzed her in through the enormous wrought-iron gates, and Grace jogged into the storybook grounds of Elliston Manor.

A small path shrouded by a thick canopy encircled the manor, and even in a flash storm only a trickle made it through the dark green overhead. She walked around to the back of the main building, then turned into the dense woods that marked the edge of hotel grounds. After a few minutes, she stepped into a clearing and onto the front porch of a two-storey timber-frame house.

Eunice's nurse was waiting for her in the entryway, thinner than ever, eyes sunk deep into their sockets.

"Is that Grace?" The nurse flinched at the throaty call from another room. He looked at Grace with wide eyes.

"Yes, it's me. Got caught up this morning, pushed everything off schedule."

"Can I take your coat, Ms. Hart?"

"That's alright, thanks. I've got it. And please, call me Grace."

"Tell the boy to take the rest of the day off." Eunice's voice croaked into the entryway again. "Don't need him rattling around in this weather anyhow." Grace smiled as gently as she could at the trembling nurse.

"I'm fairly certain he has ears, Eunice. And he looks delighted at his newfound afternoon off."

—Why are you like this?

—Like what?

—Here. Alone.

—I find it painful to care about people when they're too close to me.

—Isn't that the point?

—Jesus, wise beyond your years, I see.

—Ha.

—You're right. But I think mostly I hurt the people I love.

—Why don't you stop?

—I came here, didn't I?

Eunice's library was as magical as she was wicked. As far as Grace could tell, she was the only person other than the nurse who ever set foot in this private house. As town lore would have it, Eunice hadn't been inside the manor since her husband died more than two decades ago. A different kind of alone. Grace wondered which was worse.

"Any progress with the Braille, Eunice?" she asked as she settled into an ornate wingback across from Eunice and the urn. The woman snorted, kicked the antique coffee table between them.

"Carry on from right where we left off, Grace." Grace picked the book up off the table, leaned back, and began to read aloud.

—I think you're wrong.

—You're not the first. About what?

—Hurting the people you love. I think you just care more than anyone knows what to do with.

—What makes you think that, O Wise One?

—I read your books. They hurt, but not on purpose. Just like they show you the hurt that was always there. And that's

not bad, or mean, I think that's just about the kindest thing you
can do for a person: make them feel.

By the time Grace had walked back across town to the
bookstore, the shop had closed for the evening. She
dropped more coins in the low parking meters on the
way, tucked a twenty into the wipers of a ticketed mini-
van. As she turned into the alley, she grabbed the
sandwich board from the corner. She knocked lightly on
the door before trying the handle. Unlocked, of course.

The owner himself had moved away more than a
decade ago, leaving the store in the care of his son. With
a heart for books and no mind for business, he had let
the bookstore morph into something almost mythical:
part unofficial library, part second-hand bookstore, part
event space, part bistro, occasional bar, and B&B as
needed. It was one of a handful of stops Grace remembered from her tours across the country. It was what she
ran to when she finally had to run. It was home.

She leaned the sandwich board against the wall near
the door and pulled out two envelopes from her jacket,
rested them on the counter. The owner waved from the
back room.

"Sorry I'm late, got caught up with Eunice again. That
last recommendation you gave her is such a black hole,
we go in and get lost and I come out and just have no
idea where I am. Perfect, as usual. You never miss."

"You know I had the best teacher. I've got your books here—"

"That's alright, I'm after hours here. I'll come by while you're open, just wanted to drop those off."

"You're too good for us little folk, Grace." Grace shook her head. "Drive safe. Don't know what we'd do without you."

The drive out of town was perilous: deer, after the rain; an overturned station wagon with Ohio plates; a familiar signpost knocked flat from the storm. Home, read, coffee. A message from Jim on the machine: *Gracie, hope this gets you before you head over, listen—my son says he's coming out from the city today, so let's rain check (ha ha). See you tomorrow.* A note in the agenda for tomorrow: *Jim's son cancelled? Bring reinforcements?* Settle for a cigarette.

—and here it was again, dusk, fog, pinks and greys and shadow, and she didn't turn the lights on yet, and she closed her eyes in the darkness. Here it was again: the locked drawer and the pistol, the locked drawer and the word processor. Tomorrow would be Thursday: drive to the ranch, bring meals for Betty, buy dog food for Jim, drop books at the school. Tomorrow, the fifteenth: mail the cheque for the hospital.

She set the pistol on the desk. She turned on the lights. She set the word processor on the desk. She wondered if today would be the day.

—Can we talk about Olu?

—Didn't the school year end? When is this thing due?

—Oh my god, Miss Hart, I handed in my assignment months ago.

—Oh.

—What really happened?

—How old are you, Jada?

—Seventeen.

—Seventeen. Okay. What really happened: I took everything from him, and didn't give anything. I took him for granted, every single day. The way he loved me, so cautiously and patiently and kindly, so much better than I deserved. And the thing is, you can't love someone else to make up for not loving yourself. I thought maybe if I loved him hard enough it would make me good, like maybe I would deserve him then, but nobody can live up to that. I didn't just blame him for what I hated about myself, I turned him into those demons. And once I'd poured it all into him, after I made sure we hated each other as much as I hated myself, I cheated on him.

—Jesus.

—I wish I could say I learned from my mistakes, but I didn't. I just sabotaged everything I had until there was nothing left but to run away.

—Here.

—Alone.

Epilogue

*E*va stood at the podium and imagined she could hear Dev's soft breath in the back of the lecture hall. Dev had long since stopped attending her lectures, but she was always there in her mind's eye: the tweed blazer and dark jeans, the loose, cream-coloured blouse, long legs crossed and hands folded in her lap, manicured hands toying with her rings. They would arrive thirty minutes before students were allowed in and Dev would guide her through the hall. They would stand together at the podium, Dev behind her so she could slide her arms around Eva's waist, rest her chin on her shoulder. She would kiss the back of Eva's neck lightly, nestle her forehead gently into Eva's hair, then unwind herself and settle into the seat at the back right of the hall.

Eva still arrived thirty minutes early, still walked through the hall, still felt Dev's hands around her at the podium. Now, a member of the department would come greet her ten minutes before doors opened, introduce themselves, bring water. She used to listen to the hushed conversations as students filed in, but now she let the sound of her own breath—of Dev's imagined breath—fill her ears until the lecture began. She did not need to hear, for the hundredth time, how uncanny it was that her eyes tracked movement just like a seeing person's eyes; she did not need to hear that she looked just like her pictures; she did not need to hear the infinite musings of *how does she . . .*

She always sends the department a short bio for her introduction, and they always read the long one from her website instead, so she waits, and she feels Dev's kiss on the back of her neck.

And she begins.

"As it turns out, a movie is just a catalogue: a list of feelings you want to transfer from one place to another. Your movie is a catalogue of everything that made up every moment of your story. Your movie is the way her hair was still wet, the way her shampoo filled the air when your phone rang—the ringtone, the way it got stuck in your pocket—on the day you got the news that changed your life. Your movie is the way the wind rattled the window so loudly that she had to move her lips—

warm but chapped—right next to your ear—flushed—and her breath was hot when she said 'I love you,' it's how you could see the pomade in her hair, how softly your cheek brushed against hers when you closed your eyes and whispered in back.

"Your movie is a catalogue of the touches, smells, textures, glances, scents, colours that define the feeling. You likely already know this: you craft it diligently, I'm sure. But what I'm telling you is that you don't need to create it, you need to notice it. That, I know now, is what separated my loved films from my cherished films. People—all of us—already have what we want to see, and you can show your watchers where they have hidden it. It's up to you to respect stories enough to craft what is, not what you wish or presume to be true."

*O*lu sifted through the mail his wife had left sorted on the kitchen island: bills and junk, agency mail, and a few personal letters. His wife had already taken her letters from their shared PO box, but occasionally a particularly dedicated artist would track down his personal mailing address to send a query. Unless he recognized the return address, he would usually toss them directly into the recycling, but there was a familiar scrawl in the pile today, a scrawl that clenched a fist around his throat, a scrawl on an envelope with no return address. His wife had left a few hours earlier to take their daughter to a soccer tournament out of town, and Olu pulled a bottle of gin from their liquor cabinet. He did not get a glass.

The letter was stained with coffee, with bourbon, was flecked with burn marks, was smeared with Grace's blood.

Dear Olu,

I'm sorry to be sending this after so many years. I have written and burned this letter so many times—I know it's not a letter for you, it's a letter for my guilty conscience, and that's a conscience that hasn't been your problem in decades. I'm not sure what will make this letter different, if it does make it to you. I'm not sure if I'll finally make the wrong call and drop it at the post office myself, or if my dear, well-intentioned postman will believe he is doing me a favour and take it from the porch for me before I can change my mind. Either way, I'm sorry it's made its way to you. In my right mind, I would never send this letter. And if you are in your right mind, you'd be right to destroy this. I'm sorry to have made it your responsibility.

You were right. You were always right. Artists—we can't wait to die.

And I know it isn't harder—it isn't harder to get to do the thing you've always wanted to do, to make a great living off a few books. I know what we have, what I have. A lot of good luck, unearned celebrity. I know what I am, and I know it's not harder, but being this means that I have to sit *with the horror each of us normally gets to face at our own pace. That feeling of not being good enough, of not deserving what you have, that sudden fear of letting someone down, that unexpected resurgence of memory, of humiliation. The moments fabricated from throwaway comments and cruel ex-lovers, the moments we pray will be fleeting—my writing asks me to stay there. In the first time you got dumped, in the first time you wondered if you were unlovable, in your dad's funeral, in your mom's alcoholism, in everything that broke you open every time you thought you were done being breakable. Imagine staying there, in those moments.*

That's the thing about all that blood. It wasn't just a story. It's the worst parts of who I am, distilled over the hours and days and weeks and months of my worst self. I never get to be away from who I wish I wasn't. I know you wished it too, that I wasn't her. I know we both wished for the relative calm of between-books Grace. Fuck, even the manic, egoistic, post-award Grace would do, crazy as she is. But there are too many of us. There is too much Grace, and she's a fucking nightmare. I knew it, I always knew it, I knew exactly what I was doing at every moment. I wrote it. I was unlovable and you loved me anyway, and I was set on proving you wrong.

I was unlovable, but without this worst version of myself, I don't have books. So I know it isn't harder. I know my life is easier than most people's. But I get paid to stay in the hard parts of it long enough to make sense of them. And you had more patience for it than I ever did, but you never got back what you deserved. "I'm sorry" is not enough, here, for you, it has never been enough, but I am. I am sorry, and I have wanted you to know that you were right, you were always right.

Every day I have wanted you to know you were right, and that I'm sorry.

I never loved you the way you deserved. I never loved you the way you loved me. I never loved you the way I loved the way it felt to write too long, to wonder if I would die, to wonder if I could stop fighting.

I may have never loved you, but the way you loved me changed my life.

I know you're well, and I'm glad.

Grace.

*P*aige's graduation cap rested in their lap while they stared out the passenger side window. A smile tugged tentatively at the corners of their mouth and their leg bounced gently, the cap's tassel dancing. They turned abruptly toward Finn.

"You swear I didn't seem nervous?" Finn smiled widely and shook her head.

"You were perfect, baby. The best valedictorian that high school has ever seen. Any high school! I am so fucking proud of you," and laughter from both of them filled the tiny car, spilled out of the windows, laughter that carried the end of a beautiful, terrible era. As their shared laughter quieted, Paige's leg resumed its bouncing, and Paige picked absentmindedly at a corner of their bandages that had started to come loose. Finn risked an olive branch.

"Are you excited to play at the afterparty tonight?" she asked.

"Honestly, I'm just so fucking *nervous*, Mom. Why am I so nervous?"

Finn wasn't sure if it was a question she was meant to answer, but Paige stayed silent, and hadn't turned their head away while they spoke.

"It's a terrifying thing, to care about something," she said.

"It's not like it's my first show, though. I always care about the performance, I don't get what's so different about this." Finn nodded and glanced over at Paige, that soft face so open behind the layers of high school grit and punk volition.

"It's not that it's terrifying to care about the art, though— your music is just you, it's your blood and bones, it just *is*. I'm not sure you could be scared of that even if you tried to be. It's terrifying to care about people, and the people aren't strangers this time. Lucky for you, they already love you. So be nervous, be human, but be absolutely assured that this will be the first best show of your life."

Paige stilled beside her, and out of the corner of her eye it looked to Finn like Paige's face furrowed slightly.

"The first best show of my life," they whispered, nodding. Their leg started bouncing again, and they started to chew their thumbnail. A Mick Archer song started playing on the radio, and Finn reached for the volume knob.

"I love you, baby," she said, drowning out her own voice while she cranked the dial. Paige grinned and closed their eyes, matched their bouncing leg to the bass drum, and let their loose fists start tapping out the heart of the song.

Finn knocked loudly on Paige's door and pushed it open slowly after a moment. Her knock and her voice were lost in a cacophony of punk music and shrieking. One of Paige's friends noticed her and waved, turned the music off from their phone.

"Y'all look amazing already," she said to the teenagers gathered in the room. They each twirled in their after-party getups, from a thrifted vintage prom dress to a steampunk suit to fishnets and Doc Martens. "I wish I'd been half as cool as you guys when I was finishing high school. Someone explain to me how I made a kid as cool as Paige, right?"

She tried to keep her heart out of her throat as she made sure they all had their phones charged to a full battery, that they all had her number saved in their contacts, that they knew they could call her no matter what. She confirmed that she would be ready to pick them up whenever they needed her, no matter when. She told them to keep each other safe. She told them she loved them, and Paige shooed her out of the room with a tackle that was at least thirty per cent a hug.

Once the teenagers had gone later that night, the house was empty in a way she hadn't known before. It was empty like a tree in winter: empty and a skeleton of itself, sharp-empty, dead-empty, but living and breathing in its bones. Empty with a promise of spring.

But winters are long.

In her office, surrounded by the pressing loneliness of the house's winter, she rested her hand on the locked drawer of her desk, which she had not unlocked in eighteen years. The metal handle was cool against her fingers. It unlocked easily and she was surprised that it unlocked at all after eighteen years. She moved her fingers over the tools in the drawer with the familiarity of a lover, tracing the jars, cases, handles, and blades with a soft touch, with her eyes closed. Finally she rose from the desk to cross the room, pulled a heavy metal case out from the back of the closet; spread a drop sheet on the floor, snapped in the legs of the easel, set out the kit of jars and brushes.

The scalpel was cool against her chest, and here it was again: the pain, fresh as it had ever been and tenfold, a hundredfold, carrying now a love that broke her open every time Paige smiled, a love that set her skin on fire when she could see all of Paige's firsts tangled up in that angry teenage body they tore through the world in. Why had she stopped? Because she'd been happy, because she couldn't breathe, because she wanted to let her heart beat uninterrupted in her chest while she fell in love, first with him and then with Paige. Because slicing through scar tissue is harder than slicing through stitches. Because once her chest had closed, she was afraid to open it back up again. Because there was so much more to lose, now.

Finn slowed her breath and listened to the way it filled her belly, the way it pushed her ribs out, the way it emptied her. She listened to her heart, slow and steady, the same heart that beat in Paige's chest, the same blood that spilled every time they sliced themselves open. Letting her chest heal had not stopped the hurt, of course. But letting herself love had transcended it, in Paige's first words, first steps, first crush; love had amplified it, in Paige's first heartbreak, in their first funeral. The hurt was unavoidable, of course, this hurt of being alive, of wanting and caring and fearing.

The tissue of her chest was warm against her fingers. She thought, for the first time, that she might be able to find the love in all this blood.

Acknowledgments

It is still unbelievable to me that this book exists. (That you are reading my acknowledgments!) There are a few people without whom I and this book would not exist, and I owe them a lifetime of gratitude. For now, I have the acknowledgments of my debut book, and I hope you will forgive me for indulging my own sentimentality. If I ever write another book, I promise to be more brief in my thanks.

Suture took almost the entirety of my twenties to write, and I became a dozen versions of myself as I wrote. I wrote it for me, and I wrote it for my teenage self, and I wrote it for a self I hoped to become, and I wrote it for a self I'd never imagined I would be. I wrote it for you: may it be the book you find yourself in, may it be the book that shows you a way out. I wrote this book for you.

I am so grateful to Jay and Hazel for believing in me and this novel, for teaching me everything I know about books, and for showing me exactly what kind of person I want to be.

Suture would not be what it is without Malcolm Sutton, who graciously and patiently guided me through the process of turning a pile of stories into a novel without ever telling me what to do. I have learned so much, and I am a better writer for it.

Ailsa Bristow was one of my earliest and only readers, and her eyes on these stories as they grew was invaluable as I started to think that maybe they could one day be a book.

And I am forever thankful for every kind person, team, journal, and organizer who supported my writing in any way, who encouraged me, who gave my work a chance. Thank you especially to the publishers who supported my work through the Ontario Arts Council Writer's Reserve grant program, and to the jury at the Toronto Arts Council who awarded me my first ever creator's grant to work on this manuscript.

My brother has been a consistent surprising cheerleader in my literary endeavours, and I am so lucky to have someone who will learn about a community he really doesn't care about just so that he can keep showing up for me.

My parents have loved and supported me through every ridiculous phase I went through, and they have been so patient in waiting for me to land exactly where I needed to. Their love and loyalty gave me everything I needed to find myself, and they never rushed me, for which I am so grateful.

Mikhail: I hope you make it this far, because on many occasions (and with no idea you were doing so), you literally saved my life. Boxing was my lifeline for many impossible years. Thank you.

Lesley: look at us now!

And finally, I will forever owe an immeasurable debt of gratitude to Jess, my sweetsoft heart, who infused life into this book in its final stages by showing me what love is supposed to feel like.

About the Author

Nic Brewer is a writer and editor from Toronto. She writes fiction, mostly, which has appeared in *Canthius*, the *Hart House Review*, and *Hypertrophic Literary*, among others. She is the co-founder of *Frond*, an online literary journal for prose by LGBTQI2SA writers, and formerly co-managed the micropress words(on)pages. She lives in Kitchener, ON, with her partner and her dog. *Suture* is her first book.

Colophon

Manufactured as the first edition of
Suture
In the fall of 2021 by Book*hug Press

Edited for the press by Malcolm Sutton
Copy edited by Melanie Little
Proofread by Charlene Chow
Type + design by Ingrid Paulson

Printed in Canada

bookhugpress.ca